Magic C.A.S.E.S: A Rocky Start to the Year

To : Barbra

Dreams DO Come True!

♡ Donna Simmons

Written by Cristiana N. McGuire

To those who doubted me, those who
encouraged me, and those who inspired me.

WARNING: If any of the following applies to you, DO NOT attempt any of the spells, curses, potions, incantations and whatnot, EVER. NO EXCEPTIONS.

If YOU:

- ARE NOT born into a family of magicians
- DO NOT have a spell casting license
- DO NOT have a flying license
- ARE NOT above the age of 18
- DO NOT own a WAND, SPELLBOOK, OR BROOM STICK with a receipt of YOUR PURCHASE or verification that it was purchased FOR YOU

Introduction

If you are reading this, you are likely a human, so let me warn you. What you are about to read is based on real events that may have taken place near you. If that is the case, do *not* try to get involved. Keep to yourself and try to live a healthy life. As a member of *Magic C.A.S.E.S.*, my fellow members and I will be explaining just about everything there is to know about us witches and wizards.

Many decades ago, we were known as good magicians. To avoid confusion from your show magicians, we became modernly known as sorcerers. However, many sorcerers are those kinds of magicians. Several of our own parents are show magicians, and they celebrated our birthdays on Earth with magic shows. It was pretty standard, actually.

Another thing to clear up is the fact that our civilization is pretty much built upon your atmosphere, but we are NOT causing your global warming. In fact, we *need* your ozone layer. Since we live in the troposphere, your layer of atmosphere closest to Earth, the ozone layer, is our first line of defense. Wait, you didn't know there were multiple layers of your atmosphere? Well, now you do.

All of our transportation flies or hovers. Our houses, roads, buildings, and sidewalks are all pretty much built on or made of clouds. Sometimes, when people or families are angry, their emotions cause rainstorms; but our hats' colors will tell you our moods anyway. Usually, the Weather Sorcerers control when it snows, but we don't control the significant tsunamis and hurricanes. We also keep our civilization practically invisible to humans like you, so when airplanes go by, you only see clouds. In some cases, they see storm clouds if they get too close.

Ancient, dark magic has been altering Earth's magnetic fields. Asteroids have been drawing closer and closer to Earth, and it's up to *Magic C.A.S.E.S.* to find the source and stop it before it's too late.

~Magic C.A.S.E.S.

CHAPTER 1

Charlotte

Everything started on my first day of seventh grade at St. Smithens Sorcerer's Academy. Some ear-splitting noise interrupted my peaceful dreams. I groaned in exhausted disappointment as I realized it was Monday, and summer vacation was over. I slowly sat up in my bed, took a long stretch, and turned around to put on my fuzzy cat slippers. I didn't feel my slippers on the floor at first, so I peeked over the edge of my bed. I not only found my slippers but also found my bed floating a good two feet in the air. I happily jumped out of my bed and headed for the kitchen, only to run straight into the shut door. I rubbed my sore nose and went back to celebrating the fact that my levitation spell worked!

I regained my balance, and frantically searched for my glasses, all the while my hat's alarm continued blaring. Once I finally found my glasses, I pinched the tip to turn off the alarm. I put on my slippers, tossed on my hat, and dashed downstairs to greet my older twin siblings, Amber, who was trying to make scrambled eggs without magic, and Bryan, who was reading some kind of book.

Amber had been wanting to practice cooking the "old fashioned way" for the past year, ever since she'd gone to school on Earth. This was pretty strange considering witches had seldom been without magic, but I decided it was better not to say anything.

As much as she hates to admit it, Amber can hardly cook without magic. She couldn't crack the eggs without smashing them whole, or scramble what was in the bowl without spilling it on her favorite green apron. There were globs of yolk and cracked shell all over her purple polo uniform shirt. The only things she managed to keep clean were her skirt and her black heeled boots.

Bryan, on the other hand, was sitting at the kitchen table with his nose in his spellbook, studying for his Sorcerers Exam. To be honest, I prefer studying spells over the sorcerers, but who knows? Maybe students will be studying about me and my legendary spells someday!

"Calm down sis," Bryan told Amber without looking up from his book, "or you'll be able to cook those eggs on your head."

Amber's hat was bright red, and you could see it smoking. She was so mad that her hat was burning with frustration. She took off her hat and fanned the air with it, trying to cool it down without burning her fingers. I plopped into a chair next to Bryan. When he didn't look up, I gave him a light, playful punch on the arm.

He looked at me with a jolt, momentarily turning his hat bright yellow in surprise.

"Hey, Charlie!" he said, clearly happy to speak with a calm witch, "How'd the spell go?"

"It worked perfectly! I might even be able to present it to a spell clerk and get it licensed! And please, for the hundredth time, don't call me Charlie."

"Have you tried it on anything else?" he continued, ignoring me. "How about a person? On Dawn?"

On cue, Dawn walked into the kitchen. She saw me and ran straight for my chair. Then she rubbed herself against its legs and purred to get me to pick her up.

I sighed, "No, not yet. I'll do some more tests when I get

back from school."

I could feel my hat getting cold as it turned blue with disappointment.

"Way to rain on my parade, Bryan," I grumbled under my breath.

I picked up Dawn in my lap and stroked her silky black fur. She looked up at me with her big green eyes full of concern. I decided to talk to Amber, who was still trying to scramble the eggs.

"Amber, who are those for? Nobody eats eggs, remember?"

She tried to act as though she didn't hear me, but her hat turned blue. Amber had forgotten the essential details, just like she always does, mainly when she cooks. In this case, the important detail was that nobody in the house ate eggs on their own. She usually needs reminders, but I wasn't surprised Bryan had forgotten too. I hadn't reminded her as soon as I came down either, but Bryan had been in the kitchen with Amber much longer than I had, so I knew which one of us would be facing her wrath.

"Why didn't you remind me when you first got down, Bryan?" she demanded, as her hat faded from blue to a bloodshot red.

At the mention of his name, Bryan looked up from his spellbook, only to find Amber's signature stare fixed on him with an almost flaming hat on her head. I understood why she was mad, though. She'd probably been working on those eggs all morning.

Bryan tried to look away, but it was too late. They had made eye contact. He could feel her eyes practically peering into his soul, causing guilty beads of sweat to drip down his face. His pointed hat quickly turned pale yellow in fear, and both Amber and I knew it wouldn't be long before he cracked. A couple of seconds of uncomfortable silence passed before Bryan raised his hands in surrender.

"I'm sorry for not reminding you that no one likes eggs!" he stammered.

"*And?*"

"And I won't let you cook something from scratch without reminding you anything important!"

"That's what I thought."

She turned around dismissively, and Bryan sighed heavily, relieved that he hadn't had to deal with worse.

I leaned over and whispered to Bryan, "That's a new record!" I snickered, "Four and a half seconds!"

"How long did *you* hold out last time?"

"Fifteen seconds," I said proudly.

He turned back to his book, clearly ignoring me. He tried to go back to studying, but his hat turned pink with embarrassment. I'm pretty sure his face was red too.

Amber had begun to clean up the mess she'd made with a dishcloth, and I felt my stomach growl aggressively.

"Can I have some cinnamon pancakes?"

"Sure thing," she said, clearly done scrambling eggs, "but let me get cleaned up first."

She pulled her wand out of her front apron pocket, which hadn't been spared the wrath of egg goo at all. She shook it off in disgust.

"Gross!" She raised her wand, "*Tersus sursum pulmentum.*"

The kitchen filled with clouds of sparkling purple dust. When it cleared, a spotless Amber was getting to work on my pancakes. The spell only cleaned up what areas Amber needed, leaving a half-cleaned mess of eggs on the counter and floor. I was sure she would get to that later.

She waved her wand towards the pantry, and a breeze slammed the doors open. Pancake mix, what was left of the eggs, sugar, and cinnamon gracefully flew out of the pantry on a current of wind and placed themselves in a single-file line across the countertop. Then, she pointed at the refrigerator, and a large carton of milk flew out.

Amber had cast a particular telekinetic spell, that she got published, on her wand a long time ago. The spell connects with her thoughts, so whenever she wants something to go somewhere, a gust of wind takes it there.

Amber looked back at me in my pajamas.

"Go ahead and get changed for school. Your pancakes should be done by the time you get back." She turned her attention back to the ingredients and made them put themselves in a big bowl and blend.

I placed Dawn on the floor and ran upstairs. She curled up beneath Bryan's chair and meowed pleadingly, wanting some attention. I walked into my room and grabbed my spell box, a secure shoebox that holds my spellbook, from underneath my bed.

I took my wand out of my right spell belt. Spell belts are magical and can make anything fit inside its pockets by shrinking it. I guess you'd call it a magical tool belt. You can write down spells on pieces of paper and keep them inside the pockets, or you can put your whole spellbook in one. I only have some speeding spells that last different lengths for when I'm late for school, so right now, I'm saving the extra pocket space.

I stuck the tip of my wand into a magical lock Bryan made for me, turned my wand five times to the right, and felt a tingling sensation in my hand. I pulled out my wand, and the lock and chains began to glow. Then they turned into purple dust clouds that hovered around my book.

I keep my spellbook under enchanted lock and wand because if someone were to get a hold of my experimental spells, they could either publish them as their own or something could go really wrong, and something might explode. Let's just say that I would rather not have one of those happen again.

Anyway, with the lock and chains now swirling dust clouds, I had about five minutes before they solidified. I opened my book to the first page and said, "Clothing spells."

The book rapidly flipped its pages until it stopped, and several fancy-dress spells were highlighted.

"School uniform spells," I corrected.

The book began to flip its pages again, a bit faster this time until only four spells were highlighted. The four spells were: Elementary Academy Uniforms, Middle Academy Uniforms, High Academy Uniforms, and College Academy Uniforms. I studied the Middle Academy Uniforms spell, closed my eyes, recited it quietly. *"Medio schola vestimenta suae."*

I felt a whirlwind surround me and lift me off the ground. It was like a tornado of sparkling clouds. I could feel my fuzzy Dawn slippers turning into my black heeled boots with my ankle socks. Then I felt my purple and black striped pajama pants turning into my fern green skirt.

My pajama shirt was just turning into my mint green uniform t-shirt when I heard, "Charlotte! Come and get your pancakes!"

It took every muscle in my body to resist the urge to open my eyes or to even answer Amber. With a transformation spell like this, it was essential to keep my concentration. If I didn't, the spell wouldn't work.

Almost immediately after, I heard a loud *thump*, followed by a *splat* from downstairs. The next thing I knew, Dawn had freaked out and was clinging to my freshly-formed socks.

I opened my eyes, breaking my concentration, and the swirling clouds dissipated. I dropped to the floor with a startling enough *thud* to send Dawn dashing beneath my bed. My unfinished uniform faded back into my pajamas, and the dust clouds surrounding my spellbook had turned back into the lock and chains.

"Ugh!" I stomped downstairs, irritated with my sister for scaring the living daylights out of Dawn and likely causing her to break my concentration.

I felt my hat heating up, and I was just about to give Amber a piece of my mind when I noticed some peculiar things. First, it didn't look like anything had fallen. Second, Amber and Bryan looked like they didn't know what caused the *thump*. Third, one of my pancakes was on the ceiling. The *splat* must've been my pancake, but what caused the *thump*?

"What was that noise?" I asked as I eyed the ceiling pancake.

"I don't know," Amber answered while looking out a window.

"That's what we're trying to figure out," Bryan added, scanning the ceiling and walls.

"Well, whatever it was, it broke my concentration in the middle of a spell!"

I did my best to sound angry, but I was more concerned. As Dawn cautiously came down the stairs, I began to wonder if what caused the noise had damaged the house.

I decided to do a perimeter check outside for any damage or signs of what thumped. I whistled sharply, and my broomstick flew out of our broom closet upstairs.

Yes, we have a broom closet. We're sorcerers. What did you expect? A 'broom room'?

"I'll be looking outside!" I called to my siblings.

They nodded halfheartedly. With that, I hopped onto my broom and flew outside. I circled the house looking for literally *anything* that could have fallen onto the house. I checked the ground around the house. Then I decided to check the roof. That's where I finally found something: a scrawny twig that was thinner than my wand.

Things were not looking well for my investigation. I was just about to head in when something *else* caught my eye. Several displaced shingles were surrounding what must've been the biggest rock I'd ever seen on a roof. Sure it was the *only* rock I'd ever seen on a roof, but you get my point. To be honest, it was more like a mini boulder. It was a... minoulder. Yeah.

The minoulder was big enough to crush me if held three inches above my head. I wanted to bring it inside for evidence, but then I realized I didn't know any spell that would make it possible. The rock had come from nowhere. Plus, it was going to leave a massive dent in the roof when it was removed. There weren't many meteor showers in the Troposphere, so the rock was pretty concerning. Especially in the fall.

I flew down from the roof and back inside to find that my siblings had given up their search. They were both eating pancakes. Amber was eating mine since they were getting cold, but their hats were both pale shades of yellow.

"I found what thumped!" I announced, grabbing their attention.

"What is it?" Bryan asked.

"Where is it?" Amber asked at the same time.

I hopped back onto my broom and let them get theirs. Once I led them to the scene, their hats were a bright shade of yellow as though they hadn't expected a rock this big.

I figured their first idea would be to try and move the rock, so before they could reach for their wands, I told them that we should leave it, so mom and dad could see it for themselves. Plus, I warned them that we could destroy our roof if we smashed the rock.

My siblings exchanged looks, and the yellow on their hats began to fade back into their standard colors.

"We should head back inside," Bryan suggested.

"Wait, what time is it?" Amber asked.

"7:55," Bryan said, checking his watch.

I felt my hat instantly turn into a mustard yellow, and static shocks erupted from my head.

"I gotta go!" I shouted as I rode my broom straight to my room. I still had the uniform spell memorized, so I hopped off of my broom and quickly muttered it, being sure to stay concentrated now that there weren't any distractions. The purple clouds swirled around me and lifted me into the air, quickly transforming my PJs into my school uniform. Once the clouds stopped swirling, I grabbed my broom by the handle and ran down the stairs.

"Is the bus here?" I asked, nearly out of breath.

"You just missed it," Bryan said, looking out the window.

"Just great!" This was beginning to be the worst first day back ever. I hopped back onto my broom, grabbed my pancake from off the ceiling, and flew out the door.

I looked around for the bus, and I found it about ten miles off into the distance to my left. The brooms' bristles were spouting magical, sparkling, turquoise clouds.

Our school buses and cars are like yours only instead of wheels, they have two long brooms that fly. Plus, they move faster and have a magic exhaust that helps the atmosphere, unlike your automobiles.

I took out my speeding spell from my spell belt and read it out loud.

"*Celeritate incremento!*" In an instant, my broom sped off with a ZOOM. The wind whipped through my hair as I watched my neighbors' houses zip by. I had almost caught up with the bus when I felt my heart stop. I jerked my broomstick to a 180° spin and sped back towards home.

"Of course, you forgot it," I mumbled to myself.

Once I got back home, I ran inside to my room as fast as my legs would take me. I dove under my bed, where Dawn happened to be napping on my spellbook.

I slowly pulled my book from beneath Dawn's fuzzy black body. She slowly opened one of her big, green eyes, and slowly closed it back. Once I successfully retrieved my book, I shoved it into one of my spell belt pockets and hopped back onto my broom.

The speed spell had worn off, so I had to cast it again once I got back outside. The bus was so far in the distance that it looked barely bigger than a bumblebee.

Once I recast my spell, I remembered something else: no matter how fast I flew, I couldn't get onto the bus. I would have to get to school without the driver seeing me, and I couldn't be late. If I were late, mom and dad would be notified, and I was pretty sure the last person they wanted to hear from this Monday was the seventh-grade dean. If the driver saw that I had missed the bus, it was their job to report to the principle that I was technically late. Even if I got to school on time, I couldn't ride my broom to school without special permission.

I yanked the handle of my broom upwards; I flew straight up into the air. I was deathly afraid of going straight up, but it had to be done. I held onto my broom for dear life and squeezed my eyes tight. I counted in my head *One...two...*I paused. *Three!*

I shoved the broom back down, so my flight path was straight, and I was a good ten feet above the bus.

I reluctantly looked for the school, and it was about half a mile ahead of me. That's when I began to lose speed, and I realized my spell was wearing off. I was just about to recast it when I remembered that I would have to make it past the bus driver, front office staff, and everyone on the bus to successfully be on time without being seen.

Before I recast my spell, I took out my spellbook. It unshrunk from my spell belt pocket and nearly tipped my broom over from its weight. I kept flying forward slowly, and the bus seemed to pick up speed. I had to figure out how to get by everyone without getting caught; and fast. The bus and I were nearing the school.

Should I recast a speed spell? No, I'd cause smoke from my broom when I tried to speed past the bus and the front office staff. I'd have to go commando, but I would have to recast a shorter-lasting speed spell, one that I had saved in my belt. If I were to cast the longer one, it wouldn't wear off until it was too late. I found an invisibility spell and severely modified it so that it wouldn't wear off until I was with the rest of my homeroom class. That way, my teacher wouldn't see me appear out of thin air in the middle of his classroom. But by the time I made the adjustments, the bus was directly below me on my right.

I recited the complicated spell, "*Inuisibilitas manent ante liberi perveniet,*" and in clouds of magic smoke, I saw that my hands were no longer on my broomstick handle. In fact, my broomstick was gone, as well.

I looked for the bus only to find it gone too. Did I turn the bus invisible? I thought. I looked frantically to see that the bus had only flown ten feet forward and was stopped at railroad tracks. Yes, we also have trains. I pointed my broomstick downwards so that I flew right in front of the bus. I decided to recast my speed spell, which I luckily had memorized, and I put my book back.

It wasn't long before I found myself at the school's wide-open front doors. A *Welcome to St. Smithens* banner was above them, and I rode my broomstick straight through. I flew through the halls to my classroom, which I would've been in trouble for if I wasn't invisible: room 205.

The teacher was at his desk at the front of the room with nothing but a coffee mug and a computer taking up space. His rolling chair and desk hovered a good two feet in the air from the floor. He had HUGE a whiteboard in the center of the front wall reading:

Welcome back, Seventh Graders! My name is Mr. Blackwood, and I will be your homeroom teacher for the year. When you come into the room, please do each of the following:

1. Find your assigned desk
2. Find your assigned lockers
3. Get organized for the day

Once finished, you may quietly talk amongst yourselves.

I had completely missed all of the lockers in the hallway. As I began to fly back out the door, I noticed Mr. Blackwood was laughing at his computer. I hopped off of my broom, careful to keep a good grip on it so I wouldn't lose it, and looked over his shoulder. What I saw nearly made me burst out laughing.

My homeroom teacher was watching funny cat videos on YouTube.

The next clip that came up was of a little kitten in a cardboard box trying to get out. That's when I felt a tickle in my nose. It got stronger until… "*Achoo!*"

"Bless you," he said

"Thank you," I said, before realizing how dumb I was.

"You're welcome…" He said before he jumped out of his hovering seat and fell to the floor.

I almost asked if he was okay before remembering I was invisible. He hopped up and looked around with suspicion and fear. His pointed hat was bright yellow, and he was just beginning to do a thorough search of his classroom. If he was to cast a revealing spell, I was doomed.

I hopped back onto my broom and flew to the hallway to find my locker. I found mine, number 15. The lockers were long and blue, each one stretching up to at least six feet, lining the hallway. The locks had small holes just barely big enough to fit a pinky finger.

Out of curiosity, I pulled out my wand from my spell belt, once I finally found it, considering both it and my belt were invisible and put the tip into the hole. The lock disintegrated and turned to a golden cloud that hovered where the lock had been before.

I opened my locker to find notebooks, textbooks, pens, pencils, highlighters, and even a case for my wand. I reached out for the case, and when I grabbed it, it turned invisible too. I dropped it in surprise, and when it clattered against the floor, it became visible again.

Mr. Blackwood came out into the hallway. In a panic, I grabbed my wand case off the ground, turning it invisible again, hopped back onto my broom, and flew into the first room on my left. I slowly shut the door and sat down. I stayed quiet and listened for Mr. Blackwood. Once I heard him leave, I heaved a sigh of relief.

That's when I realized where I was. The seventh-grade dean's office. The office was pretty small, but it had just enough space for a desk, a desk chair, and a computer.

The dean was sitting at her desk with reading glasses on the tip of her nose. She had a strangely contorted necklace tied on a brown string that practically glowed in the dim, lamp-lit room. She was squinting at her computer, so she hadn't noticed me come in. That's when I felt a tingling sensation throughout my body. I looked at my hands and saw them. My broomstick appeared next to me, and I heard seventh-grader voices outside the door.

The spell wore off, and I heard the dean rise from her seat. Her chair wheels squeaked as she pushed her chair back under the desk, and I wondered how much trouble I was about to get into.

CHAPTER 2

Alexander

My alarm went off. I woke up and ate breakfast. Nothing unusual with my morning routine. I cast a spell to put on my uniform and then waited in line for the bathroom. My twin sister, Eliza, took forever in there. Brushing her hair, taking a shower, putting on makeup, it was always something! I told her to hurry up, so I could brush my teeth.

"If I'm gonna be an actress, I've gotta look my best!" she reminded me for the hundredth time. I tried to tell her that she's pretty on the inside, and she doesn't need makeup, but she always wanted to take her time or do it from scratch. I just don't understand how it can take so long to get ready or even put on makeup without magic. I mean, regular humans do it all the time! I bet they don't take *hours*.

"You boys just don't understand," she declared, probably shaking her head.

"Boys don't *care*, either," I muttered.

"*Excuse* me?"

"Nothing!" I said quickly. My sister scares me sometimes, and I'm the oldest! She is really nice if you can get her to trust you. Break her trust, and things don't end well. She usually acts bitter and mean, at least towards me, but in the end, we look out for each other.

Probably thirty minutes later, Eliza got out of the bathroom, so I went in and brushed my teeth. I went back to my room, grabbed my enchanted satchel off of my door handle, and reached in to grab my wand and a notecard. Reveal Spell the top read, so I said the spell out loud, *"Revelare."*

Most kids use spell belts, but my sister and I use satchels. Mine is beige leather that shrinks any object you put into it, just like a spell belt. Hers is turquoise with a glittery purple star on the flap.

My whole room was filled with magic clouds, and when they cleared, my spellbook was on my nightstand next to my bed, I usually keep it invisible, so most people just assume I have it with me. I grabbed it, tossed it into my handbag, and went downstairs.

Eliza was on the couch, making innocent faces into a mirror. I rolled my eyes and asked her where mom and dad were. She rolled her eyes and looked at me like I was dumber than a bag of rocks.

"They're at work, remember? They have to work now that we have to go to school."

Oh, right. I walked over to the front door and looked out the peephole. There were kids at the bus stop in front of us, just standing there looking at something to their left. I looked in their direction and saw the bus flying towards us.

"It's here, Lizzy."

"Don't call me that!" she snapped as she shoved her mirror into her satchel. I was kind of nervous since I didn't know anyone at St. Smithens, but I knew I would have to deal with it. If my sister knew I was scared of a new school, I would never hear the end of it.

We both rushed out the door so quickly that we both nearly fell out of the sky. I grabbed my sister's arm just before she fell off of the clouds.

We both went back inside and grabbed our brooms, and I told Eliza we would have to catch the bus at the next stop.

She rolled her eyes but hopped on her broom anyways.

We flew beside the bus until we neared the stop. Then, we got the driver's attention, an extremely overweight bald man, so he would wait for us. He rolled his eyes and picked up a walkie-talkie. When he was done walkie talking, he motioned for us to climb aboard. You see what I did there? Anyway, once we got on the bus, I stopped and almost immediately got back off.

Everyone had stopped talking to watch me and my sister get onto the bus. We slowly walked to the very back as every student's eyes followed us. I'm probably exaggerating, but that's exactly how it felt. I took the window seat, and as soon as we sat down, the kids went back to talking as though nothing happened.

I didn't feel like looking out of the window and wanted to talk, but Eliza obviously wasn't in the mood. I was going to attempt to strike up a conversation with the kid in the seat to our right, but he was a tall, muscular guy who would probably beat me to a pulp without magic. So I figured looking in his direction wasn't the best idea.

I thought about how many other masculine guys there had to be at school who were more than willing to pulverize me, so I reached into my satchel and pulled out my spellbook.

I closed my eyes and concentrated on invisibility spells. My book's pages turned and then stopped on a page titled *Transparency*. I read through the spells and their descriptions until I found a long-lasting one. Then I reached back into my handbag and pulled out a pencil and notecard to jot the spell down.

Out of the corner of my eye, I saw Eliza peering over my shoulder.

"What would you need that for?" she asked.

"Just in case. I'm not taking any chances."

She pondered the thought, then took out her spellbook. I put all of my things away and watched as her book's pages flipped. I wondered what spell she could possibly want, but I stayed quiet.

My eyes began to wander, and I found myself looking through our window. I saw what I thought was an eagle, which was pretty strange because they usually don't fly this high, but then I realized it was a caramel-skinned girl. Her dark, curly brown hair was flowing in the wind. She reached over to her right to what was probably a spell belt. She pulled a huge book out of a pocket and began to wobble. I gasped.

"What is it?" Eliza asked as she moved closer to the window and followed my gaze.

"What is she doing up there?" I wondered aloud.

"I don't know, but it looks like she's trying to avoid something down here."

She must be pretty brave, I thought.

I pointed at the girl as she raised her wand, "Look."

"Who is that?" she asked.

Before I could say "I don't know," the girl had made a massive cloud of smoke around her. Once they cleared, she was gone.

"Where'd she go?"

"Invisibility spell," my sister mumbled.

"Why?"

"Maybe because she didn't want the bus driver to see her."

I thought about that. Then I heard a whoosh from the front of the bus and saw glittery dust clouds. The same ones that had surrounded the girl before she disappeared.

"Speed spell," I muttered.

"Must be in a rush."

"Maybe she goes to our school."

"Doubt it," she said.

I was about to ask her about the spell she chose when the bus came to a sudden stop. We both slammed into the seat in front of us. Once we recovered, Eliza arched an eyebrow, and I shrugged. I looked ahead to find us at a railroad crossing. The bus got quiet again and stayed that way for a while. Once we started moving again, Eliza pulled out a hand mirror and her wand from her handbag and began to comb loose strands out of her face. I rolled my eyes and thought about the girl in the sky.

The way her curly, dark brown hair flowed through the

wind as she rode her broom. She must've been pretty brave to fly so high. I couldn't think of a single reason good enough to fly so high. I mean, sure, we literally *live* in the sky, but that doesn't mean I like heights. We used to live on Earth, but then my parents lost their magician jobs after an incident... I shouldn't go into detail. I was younger then and don't remember much.

My mind began to wander until I found myself back in reality. School. The first day to be exact, and I knew nobody but my sister. Maybe, if luck was on my side, the girl would be here today. Perhaps we could even be friends.

Then the bus stopped again, not as suddenly this time, and kids got quiet. The bus driver stood up and began a lecture. His voice was raspy and dry like he had eaten sand, and he had a strong southern accent. To be honest, I didn't really listen, but I did hear him say something about getting quiet at each bus stop until the people sat down.

"Oh," I mumbled, "that's why it got so quiet."

He went on and on, and I honestly didn't even know his name, but what I did hear was the very end.

"And you two," he pointed two meaty fingers at my sister and me, "I wanna talk to ya."

My sister and I exchanged glances as everyone on the bus turned to see who he was pointing at. My sister and I nodded at him, and he opened the bus doors at the school. We waited for everyone to get off before we cautiously walked to the front of the bus.

"You wanted to see us, sir?" I asked nervously.

"Yeah. What's your name, boy?" His breath reeked of smoke and stung my eyes.

"Alexander, sir."

"How 'bout you, sunshine?" he pointed his finger at Eliza.

She hesitated before mumbling," Elizabeth."

"What was that?"

"Elizabeth," she declared more clearly.

"What's with you two? Don't seem to be around here."

I explained how she was my twin, as Eliza told him how we'd

just moved here over the summer.

"So, y'all are from the ground?" he asked when we were done.

"Yes, sir," my sister answered.

"Well, then I'm gonna let y'all off with a warning. If y'all miss the bus again, your parents are gonna be notified."

"Yes, sir," we both said.

"Now get off my bus."

"Yes, sir."

My sister and I got off his bus.

"What a great way to start the day," I muttered as we entered the school.

When we walked in, we found the seventh-grade hall, and our homeroom, room 205. Mr. Blackwood.

We read the board and found our lockers. Mine was 17, and Eliza's was 16 on my left. I saw what looked like a lock on the door. Curiously, I looked at my sister to see if she knew how it worked. Somehow she did, and she stuck the tip of her wand into the lock. I did the same, disintegrating it.

I gasped, catching the attention of a few of my peers, then nervously chuckled and pointed towards my locker. They went back to their business as I wondered how I was going to survive the week. Suddenly, I heard a loud creak of a door. I turned to see a tall young woman with reading glasses at the tip of her nose, a business suit, a tall black hat on her head, a strangely necklace swirled, and cracked heels that made her at least four inches taller than she actually was.

I was staring at her heels when I noticed something. A shadowy figure around her ankles. When the figure poked its head out, I almost gasped. A girl with dark, curly hair and purple rimmed glasses poked her head into the light from the bottom of the doorway. I nudged my sister as the woman began some kind of speech. She turned around, annoyed, and followed my gaze.

Eliza turned white when she saw the girl, but I couldn't imagine why. I mean, she should be happy to have such a brave and probably smart girl at our school.

The dean introduced herself as Ms. Apopano and went on with another lecture that I didn't really listen to. I had my eyes glued to the girl as she cautiously looked around before scampering out of the dean's office.

I started to call out to her, but then I remembered that I didn't want to draw attention to myself. Of course, I didn't realize this until *after* I called out to her just as the dean started to wrap up her speech. Eliza elbowed me in the ribs, hard, as Ms. Apopano glared at us.

"Pan and Coventina Trevil." she said slowly but sternly, "When I finish my introduction, join me in my office." How in the air she knew our middle names was a mystery to me.
When she finally finished, Ms. Apopano went into her office, and everyone else went back to their business. We followed her into her tiny office and stood there awkwardly since the only other chair was at Ms. Apopano's desk.

"So, you two think you can just casually interrupt my introduction speech?" she asked.

"No, ma'am. Not at all." Eliza reassured her, "You see, my brother saw a student trying to play a joke on you. He caught their attention just before they played the prank. I saw him too. The student was going to plant a fake rat at your feet." I looked at my sister, mystified. I forgot how good of a liar she was.

"Oh, save it, Coventina. Like you or your brother would ever save me from anything. Don't think I've forgotten what your ancestors did to me. I will get my revenge. They may be gone, but you're still here." She sent shivers up my spine as she spoke.

"You are dismissed, but this is not over." She waved her hand, and the door opened, so we walked out. As soon as we left, the door slammed behind us. I thought I heard her say something about a present not being delivered from behind us. My sister and I looked at each other and just shrugged. I wasn't sure what our dean was talking about. Maybe somebody put too much cream in her coffee, but she was definitely crazy.

Even though I was still a bit shaken up from our encounter with the dean, I began to look for the girl. When I couldn't find her by the time the homeroom bell rang, I began to lose hope. I started to fear that she was gone for good as I entered our homeroom classroom.

I sat in my assigned seat and put my head in my hands, my mind racing with questions. *Where could she have gone? The school isn't that big... Is it?* I was so deep in my thoughts, I didn't hear the teacher call roll. Eliza had to elbow me in my ribs. Hard.

"Ow! Hey!" I snapped before noticing everyone glaring at me.

"H-Here!" I said, as my hat turned light pink with embarrassment. The teacher rolled his eyes and moved on as I heaved a sigh of relief.

"What's up with you? You seem really out of it," Eliza told me as I started zoning out again.

"I'm fine," I told her halfheartedly, "Just thinking about things."

She sighed, "Thinking about that girl, huh?"

"Maybe."

"I wouldn't trust her if I were you," she whispered.

"What! Why not? You haven't even met her!" I snapped defensively as my hat began to heat up.

"Calm down! She just looks suspicious. That's all." She mumbled something under her breath.

"What?" I asked her.

"Nothing," she said quickly enough to raise suspicion. I started to ask her some more questions when she raised her hand to be excused to the restroom. Once she was dismissed, I saw another girl walk into the room without a hat on her head.

She came over to my table, since her name tag was there, and sat down next to me. She put her head in her hands and had a far-off look on her face. I was pretty sure she was blushing, and her ears seemed a bit red. I tapped her on the shoulder.

"Are you okay?" I asked, concerned.

"Huh?" she jumped up in her seat. "Oh. Yeah, I'm fine," she said dreamily, "Just perfect," and she stared off into space again.

I sighed. *Girls*, I thought to myself. *They are just so... What's the word? Interesting. Yeah, that's the right word. Interesting.*

I decided I would try to catch her after school when it was dismissed. Maybe I'd catch up with her now that I knew what she looked like. I had just started to devise a plan as to how I was going to find her when Eliza came back.

"You still thinking about things?" she asked.

"Yeah. I'm gonna find her," I declared confidently.

"Why do you want to so badly? I think she could be dangerous. If anything, you should be thinking about how to stay away from her." I felt my hat burn in rage. I wanted to go off on her, but I knew better. The last thing I needed was to say something I'd regret.

I raised my hand and asked to be excused to the restroom. I walked out of the classroom, nostrils flaring, and went in. I took off my glasses and splashed water onto my face. I took slow deep breaths, and my hat turned back to normal.

"What is up with her? Is it so wrong for me to just want to do something? Is a little exploration really that bad?" I wondered aloud.

"You're right," someone agreed from behind me. I turned and found a wizard leaning against the wall casually, his face covered by his hat.

"A little exploration never really hurt anyone. I mean, you're just looking for answers."

I wasn't even suspicious. Just happy to hear somebody who understood.

"Yes! Exactly! Somebody who-" I was interrupted by the bell signaling the end of homeroom. I shook my head and blinked. *What just happened?* I thought to myself. *Who was that guy? Why did I feel so...trusting with him?* It had sort of been like I was hypnotized, but not quite. More like deceived into a false state of trust and security.

By the time I had gathered my thoughts, the wizard was

gone, so I readjusted my hat and headed off to first period. Still a bit confused.

CHAPTER 3

Sabrina

How should I begin? Probably with something important.

Okay. First of all, I'm a human, just like you. That's right. You can be a sorcerer as long as you have a real spellbook, wand, hat, and some kind of enchanted travel case. I have three out of four of those items. Well, I did until my grandma gave me an enchanted book bag for my first day of magic school. It shrinks stuff. I think you get the idea.

Now, I'm actually gonna start my story.

I woke up to an alarm clock, probably like yours. I yawned stretched. All of that good stuff. Then I did something I never successfully did before. I cast a uniform spell.

Here's the thing about spells. There is a precise way that you must say every syllable. Real witches and wizards are born with a natural ability to say these spells correctly, while humans like us have to try really hard. I found a spell that gives me this natural ability, but I still can't get it right.

That's why I was excited about going to St. Smithens. I could make a friend, who's a real witch, and get her to cast the spell on me! It'll be perfect!

Anyway, back to the story.

I successfully pulled off my uniform spell, just in time for school. I ran to my grandma in the kitchen, cooking pancakes and bacon.

"Grandma, look!" I said as I twirled around, showing off my uniform.

She smiled, "You finally pulled off that spell, dearest? I'm so proud of you! I bet your mother and father would be too."

I sighed, "I bet they would be proud, grandma. I bet they would."

My parents are disgusted with the idea of any kind of magic and mystical creatures. Of course, that doesn't stop them from both working in the fortune-telling business. In fact, if I even bring it up, my parents will give me some kind of task or chore to do to change the subject.

My grandma and I knew that sorcerers could be nice. Just not all of them were, but they still had their reasons. After all, grandma kept books with cool stories about the evil sorcerers being defeated by the good ones. One of them was about how the dinosaurs really went extinct.

Sorry! Got off track again!

"So... how am I gonna get to school again?" I asked my grandma.

"I know a spell that will do the trick. Now, what time does your school start?"

"8:15" I answered, having memorized my schedule.

"And what time is it now?"

I checked the clock on the wall, "7:57 A.M."

"You should eat some pancakes, dear. You still have time."

I didn't want to eat my pancakes. I wanted to get to St. Smithens Sorcerer's Academy, and I wanted to meet a real witch so I could cast spells like one. But I ate my pancakes anyway, and once I finished, I rechecked the time. It was 8:05, so I asked my grandmother again if she could get me to school. This time she nodded and took her wand out of her spell belt.

She sighed, "Alright, my sweet. I wouldn't want you to arrive late on your first day. *Sto Scholio*," and she pointed her wand at me. My vision was clouded with sparkling lights, and the next thing I knew, I was at the doorway of St. Smithens.

I squealed with excitement. I was at a real sorcerer's school! After taking a moment to collect myself, I walked through the doors.

Once I walked in, I couldn't help but stare in awe at just about everything I saw. I couldn't help but marvel at everyone's hats and enchanted travel cases. It was all so unreal! I looked around for my homeroom. Room 205. Once I found it, I went in, read the board, and found my locker, number 14. When I went out to my locker, I found everyone listening to some kind of lecture from a short woman in high heels, which clearly were just there to make her look tall. I tried to pay attention to what she was saying, but I couldn't help but stare at her high heels. It looked like she'd spent most of her life dancing in that pair because her shoes literally looked cracked. I honestly didn't know you *could* crack heels.

While I was staring at her heels, I saw a shadowy figure near her ankles. Then it peaked its head out to reveal a caramel-skinned girl with curly hair and glasses on her hands and knees scoping the area.

She was obviously hiding, but why? Maybe she was hiding from the woman, who turned out to be seventh-grade dean since she was in her office. I wanted to say something, but you really shouldn't do that when your dean is giving a lecture. As the dean continued, I watched as the girl prepared to escape. She waited until some boy caught the dean's attention before scrambling to get out of the office.

She moved so quickly that I didn't see where she went. Once the dean finished her lecture, we were all dismissed to homeroom. I went into room 205 and followed the instructions on the board. The magic lock made me yelp when it disintegrated, and I staggered backward. I tripped on something and was caught by a handsome young wizard.

"Are you okay?" he asked.

"I'm fine, I'm just not used to these locks."

"Good. If you ever need someone to catch you again, give

me a call. My name is Richard, but you can call me Rick."

"I-I'm Sabrina," I told him, pretty sure I was blushing.

"See ya, Sabrina," and with that, he walked away. I took off my bright pink hat and threw it into my book bag before going into homeroom.

Rick. What a great name for a nice boy, I thought. I wondered if he played sports, or if they had sports for sorcerers since they're in the sky. If he did, I was definitely going to be a cheerleader. I was debating whether or not to find a cheerleading instructor when I felt a sudden tap on my shoulder. I jumped up in surprise to find a caramel-skinned boy next to me, looking concerned.

"Huh?" I asked before realizing he was checking on me. I told him I was fine before going into a fantasy land where Richard and I were sitting on a cloud watching the sunset, having eaten a lovely dinner. I had slowly begun to reach for his hand when the bell rang, signaling the end of homeroom. I groaned in annoyance and disappointment, found my next classroom, and found my assigned seat with a hovering name tag above it.

I sat at a five-seater table near the same boy from before and a girl next to him with silky black hair. The two other seats were empty. The boy from before's name tag read "Alexander," and Silky Hair's label read "Elizabeth."

The other two name tags read Charlotte and Samuel. I was going to introduce myself, but the boy looked deep in thought, and the girl just stared at him with a nervous but concerned look on her face. I decided it would be best to stay quiet until the teacher, Mr. Thornheart, called attendance.
When he called Charlotte's name, everyone looked around. I looked back at the girl's desk beside me and saw nothing but a floating pencil. Wait. What?

It was heading up a sheet of paper with the name "Charlotte Parker" at the top. Then a voice came from the seat, "Here!" it declared.

Everyone was startled, and my entire table stared at the chair in disbelief. Mr. Thornheart was mystified, then he regained his composure and said, "Ms. Parker, would you please make yourself *visible*?"

The voice from the chair said, "Oh! Yes, sir! Of course," as she nervously chuckled. We heard rustling around in what I can only assume was her bag. Then the voice sighed and chuckled nervously again.

"My apologies, sir, but I can't seem to find my wand." I heard her mutter under her breath, "And I don't know the spell."

Mr. Thornheart sighed and lifted his wand, "Very well, but please try to stay visible during school hours. *Revelare*."

Turquoise clouds drifted through the air from his wand to the seat beside me. Swirling around and covering the chair altogether. Then they dissipated, revealing the caramel-skinned girl with curly hair and glasses from before.

"Now, I don't want to catch any of you children invisible in my classroom again, but since it is the first day, I won't send you to your dean," he commanded sternly with his wand pointed at Charlotte.

She slumped in her seat, her hat turning pink with humiliation and her face turning bright red. "Yes, sir," she mumbled as she stared at her headed sheet of paper. Elizabeth elbowed Alexander and whispered something in his ear. He gasped and whispered something back. As they continued their quiet conversation, Mr. Thornheart called Samuel Phillips. Everyone at our table looked at the empty seat, heading the table. Then, a huge smoke cloud appeared, and a voice said, "Present, here, and accounted for."

As the clouds dissolved, a cute wizard with scruffy black hair appeared leaning back in his chair, hands casually behind his head. Mr. Thornheart stomped his foot in outrage.

"Is this some kind of a joke?" he bellowed as his hat turned bright red, "It isn't funny! I see nobody laughing!"

Samuel looked confused and a bit frightened by his teacher's sudden rage.

"No, sir! I was just having some difficulties finding my classroom, so I cast a spell to get me to the right one." He had his hands up as though surrendering, and his hat was kind of yellow. Mr. Thornheart's hat returned back to normal, and he sighed.

"My apologies, students. It has been a rather long morning. Let us continue with attendance." He glared at Samuel, and we went through role without any more surprises. Alexander and Elizabeth kept at it with their little conversation, but Alexander seemed less into their discussion and more interested in Charlotte. She had her arms crossed and her head in them on her desk. Her hat was wrinkled now and still light pink.

I tapped her on the shoulder, and she jumped up in surprise.

"Sorry!" I apologized quietly, "Just wanted to see if you're okay."

She sighed, "I'm fine. Just a bit embarrassed is all," she chuckled. "Well, I guess this day's off to a pretty *rocky* start."

I gave her a confused look, and she whispered she'd tell me about it later while pointing at the whiteboard. I looked up to discover that Mr. Thornheart was writing instructions on the board. Well, technically, he wasn't writing them. A marker was moving across the board on its own. I then noticed our teacher at the back of the room. He was waving his wand as though he was writing in the air.

The board read:

This will be your Creative Writing class. Your first assignment will be to spend the rest of the class period writing an essay about your fondest childhood memories. If you finish the task early, then you may whisper amongst those seated around you. If you do not finish today, you will complete the assignment tomorrow. Tonight's homework will be to bring in a silent reading book, write a paragraph about the book you plan on bringing, and why you chose to bring it.

In reality, it would have taken a long time to write this by hand, but magic is a lot quicker than any human hand. He had it all written in a matter of seconds. Charlotte started right away, while everyone else searched for sheets of paper. Elizabeth, Alexander, and I didn't have any, but everyone else came prepared. Samuel saw our dilemma and took out a sheet of note-book paper, raised his wand, and quietly said, "*Tres effingo.*"

The paper lifted itself off the desk and dropped a new sheet in front of each of us. Then it drifted back in front of Samuel.

I mouthed him a thank you, and he winked and gave me a thumbs up. Elizabeth did the same, but when she received her thumbs up, she blushed. Alexander just stared at her, like she had some strange disease, and just smiled and nodded at Samuel. He did the same, and we all started our assignment.

I wrote about growing up in my parents' fortune-telling shop. How my mom would teach me how to read palms while my dad showed me how to interpret horoscopes. I almost wrote about how my dad taught me to be wary of all witches and wizards, for they would bring the end to us all. Instead, I wrote about how my grandma kept ancient books of sorcerer's history from as far back as the dinosaurs. I wrote about the most recent tale I had read. The story of a woman named Katara Apopano who killed all of the dinosaurs using an army of asteroids.

Once I finished, I looked around to find everyone else at my table finished too. We all just looked around in uncomfortable and awkward silence. Then, finally, Elizabeth broke the ice.

"So...Charlotte. You made quite an entrance today."

Charlotte turned bright red, and her hat turned pink.

"Um...yeah. About that... It's kind of a long story."

Samuel looked down at his wrist, "We've got time. Another twenty minutes of class to be exact."

"Wait, you've got a watch?" I asked, surprised that sorcerers would use them.

"Um. Yeah, I got it from Atlanta. We're right above it, you know." He answered, as though this was common knowledge. "Have you never gotten one before?" Everyone at our table looked at me, either strangely or suspiciously. Everyone except Elizabeth, who was more interested in Samuel, but I quickly tried to turn the subject back to Charlotte.

"Anyway, go ahead, Charlotte. Tell your story. I mean, I

think we'd also like to know what you were doing in the dean's office as well."

"And what you were doing flying so high above our bus," Alexander said, turning red as he said it. I mentally heaved a sigh of relief that I'd managed to avoid further questioning. I was worried about revealing my human secret.

"Oh," Charlotte said, sinking down into her seat, "You saw me?" she said quietly.

"Yes, we did," Elizabeth said.

"Well, it started this morning while I was getting dressed..."

"Hold it!" Samuel interrupted, "I am one hundred percent lost. So, you flew above a school bus and hid in the dean's office-"

"And came to class invisible," Alexander added.

"*And* came to class invisible on *the first day of school*?" Samuel seemed a lot more impressed rather than surprised.

Charlotte nodded and shrugged, "Yeah, you've pretty much-covered everything."

"Wait, didn't you say something about a rock?" I recalled from our conversation earlier.

"Yeah. This morning, I heard a loud thump that interrupted my uniform spell and scared the living daylights out of my cat. When I went to yell at my sister for it, I found out it wasn't her. I went outside to try and find out what had caused the noise, and I found the biggest rock I'd ever seen on my roof on the roof."

"How many rocks have you ever seen on your roof?" Samuel asked.

"Only that one," Charlotte answered casually.

"That's an accurate form of measurement," he declared sarcastically.

"You're right," she hesitated, "it was about as big as the teacher's desk,"

"That's not that bad," Alexander said.

"Only three times as large," Charlotte finished.

"Oh," Alexander said.

"It was lodged in our roof, right above where my bed was. If it had broken through..." she paused.

"You would've been crushed," Alexander said, turning pale with his hat.

"Well, not really. If the rock had broken through our roof while I was asleep, then I would've been crushed. I was going to say that my bed would've been crushed. At least, I assume so.

"It really depends on where you were when you heard it, what time it happened, etc. Important details like that, but in the end, it's a good thing that you're alright." Alexander said confidently.

Charlotte smiled at Alexander, making him blush, "Yeah, it really is!"

"There's more to the story, isn't there?" I asked, remembering the bus incident.

"Yeah. I was up on the roof, investigating the rock for so long that I missed the bus. But if I got on the bus at another stop, the driver would report me to the dean."

"Oh yeah, our bus driver told us about that. He told us that he'd let us off with a warning because we've just moved from Earth." Elizabeth said.

"I cast a speed spell, and I was just about to pass the bus when I realized I left my spellbook."

We all *oh'd* sympathetically. That must've been frustrating.

"So I went back home and grabbed it. Then I got back on my broom and flew straight up in the air for a few seconds before getting ready to cast another speed spell. I realized I couldn't cast one that would last too long, or I'd be zipping around the school, so I cast a shorter one. It wore off right as I caught up with the bus."

"That's where we saw you in the air," Alexander cut in.

"I cast an invisibility spell and recast my short speed spell again," Charlotte continued.

"We saw your dust in front of the bus," Elizabeth declared.

"Then I got into the building and went to homeroom,

where I did one of the dumbest things I may have ever done in my life."

Charlotte sighed and muttered something under her breath.

"What did you do?" I asked.

"I spoke to our homeroom teacher," she said, just loud enough for our table to hear.

"Why is that so bad again?" Samuel said before pausing, "*Oh*, right. You were invisible."

"Yeah."

"What did you say to him?" I asked curiously.

"Well, he spoke to me first…because I sneezed."

"Oh. So you were just being polite?" Alexander asked.

"Yeah, but I scared the living daylights out of him. He fell out of his chair and started to search his room. But that's not the funny part. The funny part is when-"

She was interrupted by the bell signaling the end of first period. We all *aw'd* in disappointment that we couldn't hear the end of the story.

"Aw, man. We'll just have to continue at lunch," Charlotte declared as she packed up her things.

"Really?" I asked, baffled, "You mean, you'll sit with me?"

"Of course! It's not like I really have anyone to sit with anyway," she said.

"You don't?" Alexander asked, as though he couldn't possibly imagine Charlotte being lonely.

She shook her head.

"Well, we'll sit with you too!" he announced.

"Yeah. I want to hear the rest of that story!" Elizabeth said. Leaving only Samuel.

"So, Samuel, are you in?" I asked.

"Absolutely! I wouldn't miss that story for the world. Also, from here on out, I insist you call me Sammy."

"How about Sam?" I asked.

"Those names, and those names only," he insisted.

"Okay. Any other nicknames?" I asked.

"Call me Alex," Alexander said.

"You can call me Eliza," Elizabeth said after him.

"Alex and Eliza. Got it! I'll be sure to remember that," Sam said, gathering his things. "Well, it was nice to meet you all, and I guess I'll see you at lunch!" Sam said, and with that, we parted ways.

Well, at least until we went to our lockers.

CHAPTER 4

Elizabeth

Alright. You already know what happened, and I know you don't want to hear me repeat things that you've already heard. So here's what I'm going to do. I'm going to start with a quick intro, then I'll get to the story. Okay?

Wait. Why am I asking for your approval? It's not like you have any control over what I write, and if you have a problem with my style, you can stop reading. Right now.

Okay then! Now that we've got that out of the way, let's begin. As my brother already told you, I want to be an actress. The best thing about acting is that you can be anyone you want to be, and it's not lying! For example, if you were pretending to be a food critic, and you took a cookie from the cookie jar, you could explain to your parents that you were "acting." See? Though I wouldn't recommend trying this at home...Not that I've tried it, of course, it just doesn't seem ideal for anyone over the age of four.

Anyway, let's start our story with our dean's lecture. I'm pretty sure that nobody was actually listening to her speech, and everyone was staring at her shoes. To be honest, there wasn't much wrong with them. At least not size-wise. They had a fascinating design. They were stone gray, and they seemed to have craters and cracks in them. It was like they were literally made of stone.

They weren't all that strange, but it was like I was drawn to them. I just couldn't seem to look away from them. At least, not until I saw Charlotte. When I saw her face, I turned pale. Her face was one that I hadn't seen since my eighth birthday party.

Then, to make matters worse, Alex draws attention to himself. I was pretty angry. I mean, I get it, you really wanted to say hi. Still, I think that could've waited until after the dean's speech. As soon as we were told to meet her in her office when she was done, I knew I had to come up with something quickly.

That is one of my many talents. Persuasion. Sure, I didn't convince her this time, but I can be pretty persuasive. You probably would've fallen for that story yourself, but the whole 'ancestor revenge' plot got to me. I think the cream in her coffee spoiled or something, but that was definitely crazy. We didn't know anything about our ancestors.

We sorcerers don't tend to brag about our history. All of the big, cool things we've ever done have ended in disaster. Well, at least I assume so. If not, then there isn't much of a good reason to keep us from knowing. After all, nobody has told us about our history, and usually, when bad things happen, our memories get erased. So, the fact that this woman even knew about our ancestors was a bit unsettling. Plus, she made it personal. She said she'd get revenge for what our ancestors did to her. Not her ancestors, but *her*. This woman was either insane or insanely old.

Anyway, let's go to homeroom. When I sat down, Alex looked strange. His hat was rapidly changing colors, a sign of mixed emotions. I tried to warn him about the girl, but he didn't want to hear it. He was getting me angry, too, and you don't need two Trevil twins ticked off. So I went to the restroom to clear my thoughts.

I splashed water on my face and fanned off my blazing hat. I looked in the mirror and sighed, "Great. You've just ruined your hair."

I know that probably shouldn't have been my top concern, but an actress must always look her best. I pulled my wand out of my handbag and pulled it over my hair like a brush, and my hair magically straightened itself with each stroke. I happened to have cast a spell on my wand some time ago so I wouldn't have to carry a brush around.

Once I was done, my hair looked good as new, so I left the restroom and returned to homeroom. I had made it back in time for attendance. Naturally, Alexander wasn't paying attention, so I had to get his attention. Other than that, nothing to report about homeroom. First period, however, is a different story.

When Charlotte spoke while invisible, I thought she was a ghost. Then I realized she was just invisible. It was when she showed her face that I nearly fainted. No wonder she couldn't reveal herself! She was the girl who ruined our eighth birthday party, and in the end, our *lives*!

My parents were show magicians, and every year, that's what they would do for Alex and me; put on a show. On our eighth birthday, Charlotte was invited for the first time. I'm not sure why, but since she was a witch, she was chosen as a volunteer to say a spell. Somehow, she said the spell wrong and blew everything up. All of our friends' parents tried to sue ours, claiming that we could've killed someone. We were always moving from home to home, but the incident followed us everywhere we went. My parents tried to go back into the magic business, but the event kept following us. They couldn't find jobs on Earth. They searched for almost five years, but nobody would accept them. Finally, they decided it would be best to move back to the clouds, where they grew up. Alex doesn't remember all of the details. He probably thinks that a little boy did it all as some prank, but I remember everything. I knew that Charlotte Parker was the girl who ruined our eighth birthday party.

That's what I wrote about for the class assignment. I wrote about how everything changed with that one show. Obviously, I left out Charlotte. I knew it was an accident, and we were both only eight, but I still didn't trust her with any spells. I had a change of heart when she told us her story. From invisibility to speed spells, she cast them perfectly. At least, I assume so. Considering the fact that she got to school almost entirely undetected. Maybe I could trust her with a spell or two.

Of course, Charlotte wasn't my main concern. Samuel, on the other hand. Talk about gorgeous. I loved the way he casually appeared in class, not a care in the world. Plus he's a good liar. You didn't really think that story he told Mr. Thornheart was true, did you? I could see it in his golden-brown eyes. That was a total lie. I'm not sure what the truth was, though.

Wait, did you expect me to deny that I like him or something? Nah. It's just too obvious. Now, if he, Charlotte, Sabrina, or my brother were to ask me, then I would be denial. I don't want to *date* him or anything. Just be close friends, you know? That would be nice.

Anyway, I was looking forward to hearing the end of Charlotte's story. I went to my locker with Alex, but everyone else followed us. It was pretty weird until we all opened them. I had number 16, Alex had 17, and Charlotte had 15, right next to me.

As we got our notebooks out of our lockers, I had to ask her, "Do you think you could finish that story?" I took her by surprise, but when she recovered, she smiled at me.

"It wouldn't be fair to the others, now would it?"

"Fair enough," I muttered, clearly disgruntled, "but what is your next class?"

"Ms. Parias, I think," she said.

I gasped, "That's my class too!"

"No way. Show me your schedule." I showed her my schedule taped onto my locker wall, and she gasped. It turned out, we had the exact same schedule! We looked at everyone else's too. Perfect matches! All of us girls squealed in excitement, but Alex and Sam just stared at us weirdly. I rolled my eyes at Alex and smiled at Sam. Only Alex noticed the smile, but I didn't see his reaction. I was already walking to class with my new best friends.

"So...back to that story?" I pleaded.

"Oh, right! I think the boys want to hear it too," Charlotte said as she turned back towards them. They were awkwardly standing there, waiting for us to come back. It was kind of cute. Guys are waiting for girls because they just don't know what to do with themselves.

When Charlotte went over to the boys, I couldn't help but notice how my little brother was looking at her. Well, technically, he's the oldest, but literally by two minutes. He had a dreamy look on his face, but he noticed me watching him and went back to normal.

I had to hold back a laugh. My brother had a crush? When we got home, he was so *not* gonna hear the end of it. That meant I had to keep my eyes off Sam, or he'd hold that over my head, but whatever.

Alright, enough of the lovey-dovey stuff and back to the story. Charlotte came back, and we walked down the hall. Before she could even start, we were in the classroom.

"Well, I guess we can try again if we have free time in class," Sabrina suggested.

"Right," I said with disappointment. The suspense was driving me crazy. Still, I was gonna have to suck it up and get through class, whether I liked it or not. I walked into the classroom and found my assigned seat at a table with everyone in our little group. I was honestly surprised. Like are there no desks in this school?

On top of that, we were practically inseparable! We all had the same schedule, we had lockers near each other, and we all sat at the same table in every class! I had a feeling we were all going to get really close.

Nothing crazy happened during roll call, but the teacher did act a bit strange when she called Sabrina and Charlotte. She quietly chuckled like she had a secret or an inside joke. Our table exchanged looks and shrugged, not really sure how to respond. Sabrina and Charlotte shared nervous glances.

I sighed. What was up with these teachers? Everyone has acted strangely around at least one of us. Well, technically Charlotte and Sam just got Mr. Thornheart angry, so I don't think that counts. But that got me thinking back to the whole incident with Ms. Apopano. If she was getting revenge on us, I was going to be sleeping with one eye open tonight. She didn't seem like someone to mess with, so I was going to do my best to stay on her good side. Well, at least as good as you can get when someone is already seeking vengeance against you.

Other than that, she introduced herself as our Communication teacher. She said that she would be helping us work together with our peers and help us with our spell casting. Sabrina seemed especially excited about this class, and I kind of was too. Since I was pretty sure we were gonna be friends for a while, team bonding seemed essential. Although, if I'm being honest, I initially thought this would be some dumb public speaking class like the ones you humans take on Earth.

"So today, class, we are going to be working on a team exercise," Ms. Parias announced. "You will work with your table to solve a problem on the board. It will be a contest, and whoever has the most creative and effective solution wins!"

The class was pretty excited for a contest. I was too, and I had a feeling we would be unstoppable.

"Oh, right! My name is Ms. Parias." There was something strange about the way she introduced herself. Her expression went from cheery to suddenly blank. She blinked and continued. "The first problem: there is a boulder stuck in your roof, how do you remove it?"

Everyone at our table exchanged glances. Um, that's a rather specific problem, don't you think? It was pretty strange, but we brainstormed ways to solve it. At first, we all looked at Charlotte.

"Um…maybe you could shrink it to the size of a pebble and then cast a spell to fix the roof?" Charlotte suggested.

We all stared at her in awe, "I thought you never moved the rock?" I recalled from her story.

"You're right, I never did," she answered calmly.

"So when did you think of removing it?" Sabrina asked.

"Just now," Charlotte answered.

"Wait, you just now came up with that solution? Like you didn't put much thought into it?" Alex asked mystified.

Charlotte shrugged, "Yeah. I guess you could say it's my... gift...I guess."

"Woah, that's incredible," Sam beamed.

Charlotte shrugged again, and I wrote the answer down on a sheet of paper.

"I guess you know what you're gonna do when you get home," I said.

Charlotte nodded, and we all waited in silence for the next problem. I heard Alex mutter next to me, "I wish I weren't such a nerd."

I nudged him, "You're not a nerd."

He slumped his shoulders, "Well, I wish I didn't overthink things so much. I mean, look at Charlotte! She doesn't think about the diameter or weight of the rock just, 'let's shrink it.' And it makes sense! It's not just the first crazy idea that comes to her. It's just *the first* idea that comes to her."

"Yeah. Did you see the way..." I paused. I almost pointed out how Sam seemed impressed.

"What?" he asked curiously.

"Nothing." Before he could press me further, Ms. Parias called for our attention.

"Alright, children. That should've been more than enough time for you to come up with your answers. Now write them down on a sheet of paper with all of your group members' names."

Charlotte passed me the sheet of paper, and I wrote our names down.

"Now, onto the next problem! Number two: You've missed the bus, but you can't reach the next stop. What do you do?"

Okay. This was pretty weird. These problems were all about Charlotte, but I decided to give it a try, "Maybe...you could catch up to the bus on your broom. Then land on the top."

"Not bad, Eliza," Sam said. It took every muscle in my body to keep from blushing. Alex had a familiar look on his face. The look he had when he knew I said something wrong.

"All of this school's buses have sunroofs, so you would be seen," Alex contradicted.

"Well, then I'd cast an invisibility spell,"

"Before or after you landed?" Alex asked.

"Um...after?"

"Then, you'd be seen casting the spell."

"Well, than before!"

"Which spell would you use?"

"I don't know!" I nearly screamed. My hat was burning, so I took it off and set it on the table. I hated it when Alex did this, and he knew it.

I sighed, "I don't know. I just wanted to try."

"It's okay. That just wasn't the best idea, but it was a nice effort," Sabrina encouraged, and I couldn't help but smile. On the table, my hat went back to normal.

"Alex didn't mean to seem like a perfectionist, right?" she looked at him expectantly.

"Oh, yeah," he said quickly, "sorry."

I stuck my tongue out at him.

"But he does have a point, well, not really. I mean, he does, but..."

Charlotte went back and forth with herself for a minute, sort of muttering to herself, until Sam snapped her out of it.

"Charlotte?" he called, tapping on her shoulder, but she kept muttering.

"Charlotte!" he said again.

"Yeah?" she said as though nothing happened.

"Are you okay?" Sam asked with deep concern.

"Yeah, why?"

"You sort of blanked out there."

"Yeah. It was like you were arguing with yourself," Alex added.

We all nodded in agreement.

She nervously scratched the back of her neck, "Oh, yeah. I...do that sometimes."

"So arguing with yourself is normal?" Sabrina asked.

Charlotte nodded.

"It's kind of embarrassing. I'm constantly contradicting what I think and say. It's almost like someone in the back of my mind. It's like a voice that tells me I'm not doing something right. Well, that and I'm terrible at choosing sides. I was trying to encourage Eliza and encourage Alex at the same time...I just like keeping everyone happy."

"That's deep," Sam said.

So you're a people pleaser? I almost said aloud.

"Well, what happened when you had that first idea?" Alex asked.

"I try to say ideas as soon as I think of them, but it doesn't always work," she explained.

Before we could ask any more questions, Ms. Parias called our attention once again.

"Okay, class! We have just enough time for one last question: Your friends are turned to stone, what do you do?"

Okay, that wasn't as bad as the first two questions. We all looked at Charlotte for an answer. "Um...wouldn't any of you like to try?" she asked.

"Sure! We break them out of the stone by blasting it apart!" Sam suggested.

"If they've been *turned* to stone, blasting them to bits wouldn't be helpful," Sabrina said.

"Right, sorry," Sam said.

"It's fine. Any other ideas?" Sabrina asked.

Nobody said anything, but instead, we all looked at Charlotte.

"Maybe there's a potion for such a thing. Since being turned to stone would likely be a curse," she started to trail off. "Well, it would be for a person. I think. No, wait..."

"Charlotte!" we all said at once.

"Woah!" she staggered back in her chair.

Sam caught it before it fell, "Gotcha."

"You were doing it again," I told her.

"Oh, sorry."

"Now, what were you saying about a potion?" Sabrina asked.

"Well, usually potions cure curses, and being turned to stone is probably a curse."

"How did you know that?" Sabrina asked.

Charlotte shrugged, "I like to go to the library. I found a book on potions and read that they mostly involve curses."

While they spoke, I wrote down Charlotte's potions answer. Then I realized that we never solved the second problem. I decided just to write down what Charlotte had done this morning.

Ms. Parias called our attention one last time.

"Class, it is almost time to leave, so finish up your answers and begin to pack up your things. I will collect your answers on your way out."

We all began to pack up, and as we did, Ms. Parias waved her wand and said, "*Oratio.*" All of the sheets of paper made a neat stack on her desk in the front of the room. Once we were all packed, the bell rang, so we got up to leave. Just before we could, Ms. Parias shut the door.

"Wait!" she called, "I forgot your homework!"

There were groans of disappointment throughout the room, but Ms. Parias didn't care. We all sat back down in our seats. "Here you go! *Dispergat!*" Sheets of paper flew around the room and landed face down in front of everyone. I turned over the paper and read it.

"It's a survey?" I asked.

"Correct! You will take this survey to help me accurately choose your groups for tomorrow!" she answered joyfully.

"Okay..." Sabrina said, "I guess we should all answer together?"

We all gave her a confused look.

"You know, so we get in the same group?" she added.

"Ohh," we all said, making Sabrina laugh.

"You guys should learn about manipulation," Sabrina suggested, but then shook her head.

"Sorry, I didn't mean to say that. I meant...oh, never mind."

"You're starting to sound like Charlotte," Sam joked, making them both turn red.

We put away our homework and left the room without any more interruptions. Ms. Parias seemed to be giving us a strange look, but it could've just been paranoia. Nobody said a word on our way to our lockers. We were all too busy thinking. The teachers here all seemed to have it out for one of us. Ms. Parias somehow knew about everything that Charlotte had done this morning, which I thought was kind of weird if Charlotte never got caught.

Speaking of which, Charlotte seemed to be going through some rough things. She was regularly arguing with herself like she had voices in her head or something. That must be hard. Imagine, every decision you want to make being judged or criticized by a voice in the back of your mind. Always nagging you. I can hardly imagine what that's like. That alone sounds like a curse if you ask me.

Anyway, back to the teachers. They all acted kind of weird, and their names were... interesting. Oh, who am I kidding? They were pretty strange. I mean, Thornheart? That doesn't sound very pleasant. Apopano? Sounds kind of like popcorn. Parias? I wondered if she had plans to go to Paris. Okay, maybe I shouldn't be judging their last names, but they are pretty strange.

When I got to my locker, I checked my schedule. Third period was the Specials. A.K.A. the period where you don't do anything educational, such as art, P.E., band, etc. They're different each day, and today I had art. I pretty much expected us to paint with our wands or something, but our art teacher was definitely crazier than any of our other teachers.

When you walked into the room, paint brushes were floating everywhere, flinging paint on every wall. The walls were covered with canvas material reaching from the floor to the ceiling. Once Alex walked in, being the last one in, he was asked to shut the door. And of course, the door was a canvas too. In fact, everything was made of art. The tables were ceramic, and the chairs were stone statues with wooden cushions.

I know, right? That literally makes no sense. If anything, the chairs and tables should be wooden. On top of that, I'd rather not have a cushion at all than have one made of wood. They actually looked comfortable, and they had details of real pillows. It was almost like they used to be real.

"Alright, my masterworks! I am Mrs. Technis," she announced.

Again with the names! I thought.

"Everyone take a seat among whomever you feel comfortable. We will begin our first assignment, momentarily!"

Naturally, we all sat together, and the teacher seemed to notice. I swear I heard her say, "Interesting," as she walked by our table. Then, once everyone had chosen their seats, she clapped her hands together.

"Okay! It is time for you all to start your assignment!" She waved her wand across a long table at the front of the room. Fluffy pink clouds engulfed the table, and once they cleared, it was covered in massive wood and stone blocks, some lumps of clay, easels, and a stack of paper.

"Now, choose what you will use to create your best works! You have until the end of class. Begin!"

As soon as she finished speaking, a flood of students was unleashed. None of us were in any rush since most of us didn't even know what to do. Once we got to the table, there was only one of each material.

"I guess I'll do pottery," I said, picking up the lump of clay.

Charlotte picked up a sheet of paper, "I'll draw."

"I'll...paint?" Sabrina said reluctantly.

"I'll use the wood," Alex said, leaving only Sam and the stone.

"I guess that leaves me on rock duty," he said.

We all went back to our table. I decided to make a vase. It was going to be tall and thin near the top and bottom with a thickened middle. Obviously, there wasn't enough clay to do all of that. There didn't seem to be enough stone or wood for what the boys wanted to make either. I took out my spellbook at the same time as them, found the spell at the same time as them, and said the spell…at the same time as them.

"*Planto maior!*" All of our materials grew to the perfect size. My four-inch-tall lump of clay was now a good foot high, Alex's woodblock was still an inch thick, but now it was ten by twelve inches. Finally, Sam's stone block was now seven inches tall, twelve inches long and ten inches wide.

We looked at each other in surprise and then burst into a fit of laughter. I knew that if I could meet friends like this on my first day of school, that anything was possible. Even if I did have uncanny teachers to deal with.

CHAPTER 5

Samuel

Look, I know you're tired of the long, annoying intros, so let me cut to the chase. I'm Sam, and my story starts with a dream.

I was in the sky, flying next to a young woman with a long black coat and a short, red business dress with rock-like heels. It was still dark out, and the woman seemed to be in a hurry. She was flying at lightning speeds on her broom when she abruptly stopped.

"I almost forgot my little present for the Trevil twins!" She reached into her coat pocket and pulled out a pebble. She cupped it in her hands and whispered something to it. The rock hovered in her hands and began to glow. She circled her hands around the stone, making it grow bigger and bigger. It kept growing until it was big enough to crush the woman herself. I could tell that the spell she'd cast had drained her. She seemed exhausted.

"I may be a bit rusty, but it will all be worth it soon enough! Soon you shall be united with your family!" she cackled to the rock while looking at shooting stars in the sky. "Now, to find a suitable disguise…" She paused, deep in thought, and then an idea hit her. "I've got it! They'll be spending most of their time at school, so I shall be their new dean!"

She casually dropped the boulder over the roof, but it seemed to hover instead of crushing through.

"Crush them before they awaken," she said coldly before pausing. "Or just make them late for school. Then they'll be sent to me, and I can end them in person." She cackled quietly but just maliciously as before and sped off once again. The boulder hovered above somebody's house for a few moments, just waiting, before its glow dimmed. Then everything seemed to fast forward. The sun had risen, the sky was a mix of pink and orange, and the boulder was glowing. That's when the boulder struck the roof. Hard. It nearly went through, but the roof somehow managed to stay intact.

Shortly after, a small girl circled her house. Investigating. Searching for answers. She reached the roof and found the boulder. Several displaced shingles must have been what caught her attention. She went back inside and came back out with two older sorcerers who must've been the Trevil twins. They saw the boulder and raised their wands, but Before they could do anything, the girl from before stopped them by standing between them and the rock. That's when I got a good look at her. She was wearing a purple and black striped button-down top with matching pajama pants. She had long curly hair and glasses, and she looked…kind of cute.

That's when I woke up. I jerked upwards in my bed, my heart pounding. I looked over where my alarm clock usually lies on my nightstand, to find it cracked on the floor. I knew I didn't have time to fix it, that the rest of my family was gone, and that I was extremely late.

I got dressed from scratch because I didn't have time to find the spell, combed my hair, brushed my teeth, and skipped breakfast. I knew that I had missed the bus, so I found my spellbook and created a new one. I upgraded a teleportation spell so that I would get to the right classroom.

I wrote it down on one of the blank pages in the back, and read it aloud, "*Nunc ut ad genus.*"

I was surrounded by swirling clouds, and the next thing I

heard was a grown man calling my full name. I assumed he was calling attendance, so I leaned back in the chair I was suddenly in and said, "Present, here, and accounted for!"

How was I supposed to know his funny bone was broken? I made up the first excuse that came to mind and, somehow, got away with it.

Now, just to clear something up. I am not very good at connecting the dots or solving puzzles. In other words, it takes me a while to catch on to obvious things. For example, when Charlotte told us her story, I didn't realize the connection until...well, you'll find out soon enough.

Anyway, let's go back to third period. I thought the art room was pretty cool. I'd love to see art everywhere I went. Too bad we only have the class twice a week. When I got the block of stone, I had no idea what to carve. Then, Alex, Eliza, and I said the same spell at the same time, and I got inspiration. I was going to make a model of the school. I figured if you can find an incredible group of people at a school on your first day, then you go to a pretty awesome school.

I decided this school was awesome enough to have a statue of it. I leaned over and whispered to Charlotte on my right, "I need to go outside."

"What! Why?" she whispered back.

"I'm carving a statue of the school, but I need to see the outside."

"Oh, well...be careful. You don't need to get yourself into any trouble."

I winked, "No promises." She gave me a stern look.

"Fine," I turned and muttered, "mom."

She playfully, I think, punched me in the back.

"I'm *not* joking."

"Ow! Okay!" I pulled out my wand and recalled the spell, quietly, "*Foras.*"

The next thing I knew, I was outside. I whistled, and my broom appeared out of thin air, thanks to a spell I cast on it. I flew around, taking in every detail of the building. Every cracked brick, every scratched window. Everything. I drew a rough sketch in my spellbook as I flew around. Then I went back and added finer details. I was about wrapped up when I ran into Mr. Thornheart on his lunch break.

"What are you doing out here, Samuel?" he asked strictly.

"I'm doing research for our art assignment," I answered quickly.

"Then where are your classmates?"

"Um...inside."

"Then why are you the only one out here doing research, if it was a *class* assignment?"

"The assignment is to make a work of art using a material of your choice. I chose a block of stone, so I can carve a replica of the school."

He looked me up and down suspiciously.

"You're sure you weren't going to *vandalize* the school? Hmm?"

"What? Of course not! I'm making a replica because of how awesome the school is!" I insisted.

He nodded reluctantly and then dismissed me, which I wasn't sure he could do since I wasn't done "researching," and he wasn't in charge of me this period, but I didn't argue.

I raised my wand and said, "*Inrerius!*"

I appeared back at my seat with a cold sweat. Charlotte looked me up and down, squinting through her glasses. Then she nodded and went back to her drawing. I heaved a sigh of relief and took out my sketch of the school. I tore the page out and began to carve.

I had just finished up the windows and doors when I decided to check on the others' progress. I leaned over and caught a glimpse of Charlotte's drawing. It seemed to be of us five, only with a more cartoony look.

"Nice," I told her.

"Hey!" she snatched up her drawing, "No peeking! It's supposed to be a surprise! Besides, it's not done yet."

"Whoops," I said sarcastically. Charlotte glared at me and

started to raise her hand in a punch-ready-position, causing me to flinch.

"That's what I thought. You know, it wouldn't hurt for you to joke a little less." I'm pretty sure I heard her say "pun intended" under her breath. I looked down the table and saw Sabrina painting a picture with an *actual* paintbrush.

You're probably wondering why that might be strange. Well, everyone usually uses *wands* for these kinds of things. I used my wand for carving into the stone. Being magic and all, they're practically indestructible. It takes incredibly strong magic to break one. Charlotte used her wand to draw, and it can double as an eraser. Our wands are connected to our thoughts by a spell typically cast on them when we're born, so they can mostly do what we need them to. Therefore, everyone except Sabrina was using a wand for their art project. I was about to ask her about it, but then she came over to me.

"Oh, good. I was just about to ask-"

"Quick question," she interrupted, "What do you want to be when you get older, and what's your favorite color?"

"Um...an architect and lime green. Why?"

"Okay! Thanks!" and she sped off back to her easel.

I just stared at her in disbelief for a second before shrugging and going back to my carving. Once I finished, I decided I should paint it, so it looked just like the school. This meant I would be going back outside again, mostly because I was bored. This time I didn't tell Charlotte and asked the teacher if I could go to the restroom.

I went in and cast the spell, but before I went outside, I turned myself invisible. That way, if I ran into any teachers, I wouldn't have any interruptions. But that also meant I'd just be going off of memory when I got back.

Anyway, I got what I needed and went back to class, no interruptions, and once I got back to class, the spell wore off. I borrowed some of Sabrina's paints and finished my model. Once I finished, the teacher announced a five-minute warning before the bell rang. I decided to cast a spell on my sculpture so it would dry.

Once I did, I noticed Sabrina frantically trying to blow her painting dry.

"Um, you know that there's a spell for that, right?"

She looked at me as though the thought never crossed her mind.

"Oh, well, I don't know it, so do you think you could..." she hesitated, "cast it *for* me?"

"Oh, sure." I raised my wand and said, "*Siccum*." Her painting was instantly dry, and I actually got a good look. It had a silver heart in the center, and around it, there were different colored paint splatters. On the top left, it was purple with a wand, and an orb of magic sat on the tip. At the top was a navy blue splatter with a black magician's hat. The top right had magenta paint with a witch's hat and a glittery checkmark. On the bottom right, the paint was teal with a golden star. Finally, on the bottom left, had lime green paint with a blueprint.

In awe, I said, "This is incredible. What does it all mean?"

"Each paint splatter is one of our favorite colors. What's inside is what we want to do for our careers. Charlotte's favorite color is purple, and she wants to be a spell writer. Alex's favorite color is navy blue, and he wants to be a show magician. Mine is magenta, and I want to be a spell clerk. Eliza's favorite color is teal, and she wants to be an actress, and the lime green is for you since you said you wanted to be an architect."

I nodded approvingly, and she smiled. Then the bell rang, letting us know it was time for lunch. We all put away our artwork at the front of the room and headed to the cafeteria. Nobody brought their own lunches, so we all went through the line. They were serving mashed potatoes, hamburgers, and fruit punch.

Then we all found our seats. I sat in between Eliza and Sabrina. Alex and Charlotte sat across from us. Before anyone said anything, I took out my wand.

"You're not going to *eat* with that...are you?" Sabrina asked.

"What? Of course not! I'm just gonna shake things up a bit. *Meliorem!*"

With a puff of smoke, my meal changed. My mashed potatoes were now one baked potato with melted cheese, seasoned with garlic. My hamburger was now a medium-rare steak, and my fruit punch was strawberry flavored Fanta.

"Woah," the whole table said at once.

"I've got to try that," Alex said, before pausing, "What did you do to the fruit punch?"

"It's soda."

"Awesome!" he said as he pulled out his wand. That's when I noticed Sabrina and Charlotte acted hesitantly.

"What's wrong, guys?" I asked them.

"Oh, nothing," Charlotte said, "I just think I'll stick with the regular lunch."

"Yeah, me too," Sabrina agreed.

Alex put down his wand and turned to Charlotte, "Why? What's wrong?"

"I'm not a soda fan. Besides, I like hamburgers and mashed potatoes," She turned back to me, "but that's a cool spell. Maybe I'll try it another time."

Sabrina nodded, and Alex cleared his throat, "I'll pass too."

Charlotte raised an eyebrow, "Why? I thought you liked soda, and you seemed so excited. Don't miss out on something you want to do because of me." She turned to Sabrina. "Not you either."

Sabrina shook her head, "I actually want my burger and potatoes the way they are." Charlotte smiled, and Eliza cleared her throat.

"Okay! Now that we've cleared that up, let's finish that story, shall we?"

"Oh, right! I completely forgot. Where were we?"

"At the funniest part?" Eliza suggested.

"Right. I walked into the room and saw the teacher laughing at something on his monitor. I came up behind him and saw what he was looking at…" she paused for a dramatic reveal, "cat videos!"

We all stared at her in disbelief.

"So you're telling me that in his free time, instead of, I don't know, actually being productive, Mr. Blackwood watches cat videos?" Sabrina asked.

"Yep! It took almost every muscle in my body to keep from laughing," Charlotte answered.

"We have weird teachers," Eliza announced.

"Tell us something we don't know," Alex muttered.

"Hey, what's the deal with you two?" I asked, grabbing their attention. There was something I had been dying to ask from the beginning, so I went ahead and said it.

"You guys aren't …*dating*, are you?"

They both looked disgusted, and before either of them could say anything, Charlotte spoke up.

"Of course not! Isn't it obvious? They're twins!"

They stared at her.

"How could you tell?" they asked, clearly surprised. Charlotte just shrugged.

"You guys look like twins to me," she replied, and that ended that discussion.

Alex and Eliza didn't even look the same race, so I have no idea how Charlotte just *knew*.

"So…now what?" Sabrina asked.

"I guess we can get to know each other," Alex said.

We talked about our pets, favorite hobbies, favorite foods. Then Sabrina made a suggestion.

"Hey, guys. I have a treehouse at my house, so maybe we can hang out there sometime."

Everyone agreed that it sounded like a fantastic idea.

"We could meet every day after school!" Charlotte added.

We all exchanged looks to decide who would have to tell her, but she got the message.

"Not starting today, of course," she added, and everyone heaved a sigh of relief.

"I figured we could all check with our parents tonight, and then Sabrina could take whoever could go with her tomorrow."

We all nodded in agreement, and it was settled. I was honestly pretty excited about tomorrow. I couldn't wait to get home and come up with a good reason as to why I should be allowed to go to Sabrina's house.

Then I got a reality check as the bell rang, signifying the end of lunch. *Oh, right.* I thought to myself. *I still have another two periods left of school.* Luckily, lunch took up fourth and fifth. We put away our lunch trays and headed off to our lockers. I checked my schedule and saw what I had for sixth period; Transformation.

"Interesting," I said when I read it. I wasn't sure what to expect other than a crazy teacher. That seemed to be something I could count on at this point. As we walked to class, I began to think about what this class may bring. Considering the course was called "Transformation," I figured we would just be turning things into other things. For example, I expected today's class to consist of us turning rocks into apples or something.

I heard the girls in front of us talking about…who knows what. That's when I noticed Alex walking next to me. He had a dazed expression on his face, and he seemed to be fixated on something directly in front of us. I tried to see what he was looking at, but the girls were the only thing in front of us. I shrugged and kept walking. That's when I realized how long the hallway was.

The girls didn't seem to be bothered, but my legs were getting kinda tired. Of course, that *may* have been because I was a lazy seventh grader, but I like to think it was an extremely long hallway.

CHAPTER 6

Charlotte

So...I'm not sure if you remember, but in the beginning, I was almost caught in the dean's office. Somehow she didn't see me, even though my invisibility spell wore off. I got a glimpse of her face, and she seemed pretty exhausted. I guess being a dean is harder than it looks. Anyway, I looked around for Mr. Blackwood, and once the coast was clear, I made a dash for the restroom. I saw it while I was flying through the halls. How I didn't notice the mass collection of large blue lockers sure beats me.

Once in the restroom, I cast an invisibility spell again and waited in a corner for first period to start. Lots of girls came in and chatted, hiding from the teachers, but one girl came in by herself. Her hat was ablaze, but she had a calm facial expression. She splashed off her face, brushed her hair, and then left. I later discovered that it was Eliza.

After that, you know the story. I cast the wrong invisibility spell; I've made a lot of different ones, which left me humiliated in first period. I honestly was grateful for Sam's interruption, because it took the attention off of me. I did feel kind of bad, though. I mean, the teacher wouldn't have been as mad as he was if I hadn't gotten him all riled up. It didn't seem to bother him at all, though, so I didn't feel guilty for long.

For the class assignment, that I'm sure you've forgotten about, I wrote about my family's curse…Why didn't I mention it before? I guess it never struck me as relevant.

Anyway, my family is cursed because of something our ancestors did a long time ago. I think they broke an ancient sorcerer's code. My parents told me the story when I was little, so I don't remember much. All I know for sure is that everyone in my family has some sort of flaw. Mine is that I'm always second-guessing myself, and when I was little, I had lousy hearing. Especially when I was being told spells. My sister has an awful temper, and my brother gets stressed out easily. Naturally, my siblings happen to share the forgetfulness flaw too. Now, this may not seem like a big deal, but the curse is that it gets worse and worse as you get older, and one day, it's supposed to drive you insane. If you make it past this point, then the curse is lifted. Luckily, my mom made it past this point in her life, being the one who carried along the cursed genes. What we don't know is what that flaw was or how bad the experience was. Of course, my siblings and I are worried we won't make it…

Moving on! I happen to have a "creative talent" you might say. I'm just good at problem-solving, I guess. But then there's my flaw I mentioned earlier. It makes things…difficult. It's literally a voice at the back of my mind. When something important is going on, it never stops, but if I'm just having a friendly conversation, it's silent. But back to my "talent." I don't think it's a talent. I think it's a skill that anyone can learn, so it doesn't seem like I'm just *special* or something. I like to consider myself equal to everybody else.

Now, to art class. Sam saw my drawing before it was ready to be shown. Before that, he was trying to sneak out. I was honestly concerned about him. Unfortunately, he seemed like the kind of kid to get himself expelled. For some unknown reason, I felt comfortable enough to punch him in the back. As soon as he left, my hat flashed a rainbow of mixed emotions.

I was angry at myself for being so weird, scared that he would think I was weird, disgusted with myself for being so…weird.

Eliza noticed and asked me what's wrong. Unfortunately, she startled me in the process.

"Sorry!" she said quickly.

"No, it's fine. What did you say?"

"I was just checking on you. You looked troubled."

"Nothing…just thinking…"

"About?"

I hesitated then slowly said, "Sam…?"

She froze, her face blank and expressionless. Then she blinked and smiled at me.

"What about him?" her expression was vaguely familiar.

"Nothing. I just feel…" I searched for the right words, "like he probably thinks I'm… some…weirdo, I guess."

She gave me the same familiar look again.

"Why would he think that?"

"I may have…punched him, *playfully*, in the back. He's a jokester. I told him to be careful when he-" I paused. Maybe I shouldn't tell anyone that Sam snuck out, but it was just Eliza. Besides, if we were all gonna be friends, we were gonna have to trust each other.

"Snuck out."

"Wait, what?"

"He wanted to make a replica of the school, and he needed to see the outside. I warned him to be careful, and he called me…" I decided to leave out that part.

"So, right now, he's outside?"

I nodded, and she looked relieved.

"So you think he thinks you're weird because you punched him in the back?"

I nodded again.

"Oh. Well, since Sam's the jokester he is, I think he knows you didn't mean anything by it."

I realized she was right, and my nerves eased.

"Huh. I guess you're right. So what are you making?"

She showed me a light grey cylinder.

"I'm almost done sculpting. Then I'm gonna paint it!"

"I bet it'll be beautiful! I'm drawing all of us with our dream jobs, but it's going to be a surprise. I'll show you all at homeroom."

She nodded, and we both went back to work. Sabrina had told me what everyone wanted to be, which was somewhat helpful. Then I went to check on everyone else's art. Eliza's vase was now sculpted, and she was adding paint, Sabrina was fanning her painting dry, and Alex...

"Alex, what's your project?" I asked when I got to his end of the table. I must've startled him because he acted kind of nervous.

"Oh! Charlotte! I didn't see you come over."

"Sorry! Did I scare you?"

"What? No! I'm fine. You...wanted something?"

"Yeah. I was wondering what you're making, and...why there's a dust cloud around it?"

"Um, yeah. It's supposed to be a surprise, so..."

"Aw, come on. You can't even *tell* me what it is? I'll even show you mine."

I could tell he thought it was a good deal, but he stayed firm.

"I'm sorry. I really am, but I don't want to ruin the surprise."

I shrugged.

"Fair enough. I bet it looks amazing, though."

He and his hat turned pink, and I couldn't help but giggle. He turned red and threw his hat off of his head. I laughed again and went back to work until lunch.

At lunch, Sam cast a pretty cool spell, but I would really only use it if the lunches were terrible. I like hamburgers and mashed potatoes, and before you judge me for not liking soda, I can explain. The carbonation is too active for me to handle. It hurts the back of my throat and tongue.

Then, Alex refused his soda too. I would never want to make someone else have less of a good time, so I insisted he had some. Sabrina seemed to want her first meal *genuinely*, just like me.

Now, to sixth period. We all walked into the classroom and found our seats. Then, a black office swivel chair spun around, revealing what should've been our teacher, Mr. Plasmata, but instead, we saw...

"Dawn?" I said when I saw the cat.

"Actually, it's Mr. Plasmata to *you*, young lady," the cat said.

I nearly jumped out of my skin, causing my hat to turn yellow. Unfortunately, Sabrina was scared too. She ran right into a wizard, who caught her before she could fall.

"Hey," he said.

Sabrina turned bright red, which her hat obviously did too, and she stammered, "Um R-Ricky! I'm sorry, ...again. I'm so clumsy."

He brushed some hair out of her face.

"You can bump into me anytime. I'll catch you."

I didn't know it was possible, but she turned even redder. While I wondered how they knew each other, the cat heaved an irritated sigh and jumped onto the teacher's desk. Then, it picked up a wand with its mouth, and a muffled spell turned him into our teacher.

"Now, children, welcome to your Transformation class. Later on next year, you all will learn to shapeshift, but for now, you will turn other things into...other things."

We all sat down, and Sam leaned in on my left and asked quietly, "Who's Dawn?"

"My cat."

The teacher began to give instructions.

"So, with a few rocks your dean has provided, we will begin class with a few simple spells."

On my right, Sabrina turned pale, and her hat was bright yellow.

"What's wrong?" I asked her.

She took a breath and looked me dead in the eyes.

"Can I trust you with a secret?"

"Of course you can."

"But you can't tell anyone. Not even Sam or Eliza or Alex."

Somehow, that's when I knew it was serious.

"Your secret's safe."

She leaned close and whispered, "I'm…a human."

I wasn't sure what to think. It made sense. Why she used a paintbrush in art. Why she refused to use Sam's spell. Humans don't have a magic tongue; therefore, it is nearly impossible for them to cast spells.

I whispered back, "Do you…want me to cast the transformation spells *for* you?"

She shook her head.

"There's a Speech spell I need you to cast."

Before I could ask any more questions, she cut me off.

"I have an idea." She told me her plan as the teacher finished passing out the rocks, "And bring your spellbook," she concluded.

I took a breath and raised my hand to get the teacher's attention.

"Yes, Miss Parker?"

"Um, may I use the restroom?" I asked timidly. I was starting to hate this plan.

"Now? Is it urgent?"

I hate it when teachers have to make things difficult.

"Yes, sir."

"Alright, go ahead."

I swiftly walked out the door and towards the restroom. Then, I waited…and waited…and waited, decided I *really* didn't like this plan, and then Sabrina *finally* joined me.

"I think I should have gone to the restroom first," she said when she got in.

I nodded and said, "Let's find that spell."

It didn't take long, but we did have to wait until the restroom was empty. A girl came in, just as I found the spell. She stared at us suspiciously and then just shrugged.

Once she took care of her business, we got started.

"You ready?" I asked.

"I was literally born ready."

I raised my wand and read the spell aloud, *"Da eos lingua magicae."*

The lights flickered as clouds swirled and lifted her off the ground, engulfing her in a funnel-like storm of sparks and magic.

"Sabrina!"

"Charlotte? What's going on?"

"I don't know, but I don't think we can stop it!"

The clouds began to turn dark gray and spun violently. Lightning cracked one of the stall doors. That's when the winds picked up speed, and I feared they would engulf everything. I had to stop it, but as soon as I went to reach for my book, the lights stopped flickering.

Suddenly the clouds stopped swirling, the wind stopped howling, the lightning stopped cracking, and Sabrina dropped to the ground with a sickly *thud*. Almost as quickly as it had started, it had stopped.

"Sabrina!"

I raced towards her and fell onto the ground. I realized I was pretty winded myself. I tried to stand back up, but I was too lightheaded and dizzy. I crawled to her. Right now, she was more important. I had gotten her into this mess, so I was gonna get her out.

"You're gonna be okay, I promise."

I put my hand just above her mouth. She was still breathing, so I checked her pulse. It was steady. I tried to wet my hands with some water from the sink. By then, I'd regained my balance, so I put my hands on her forehead. She didn't have any extreme temperatures, so I just waited...and waited. Then, after what felt like forever, she coughed. She slowly opened her eyes and looked up at me hazily.

"Sabrina! Do you recognize me? It's me, Charlotte, I'm so sorry!"

She just stared at me until she finally said, "My throat hurts."

Then, she slowly sat up and hugged me.

"Thank you. You're the best witch in the world!"

"I think you mean, in the air," I corrected with a smile, and we both laughed. I helped Sabrina off the floor.

"I think we should see the nurse. Just in case."

I fixed the stall, but as soon as I did, my knees buckled, and I collapsed.

"Charlotte! Are you okay?"

She tried to help me up, but I shook my head.

"I'm fine, don't worry."

"I think you need to be checked out by the nurse, too." Before I could protest, she helped me up, and together we headed to the nurse.

Her office was in front of the school. When we walked in, we were greeted with a blast of cold air and a strong scent of aloe and mint. A short woman in a white nurse's outfit sat at a desk facing away from the door. The moment we walked in, she said, "Pass?"

Shoot. I hadn't thought this far ahead.

"Ma'am, I found her in the restroom. I think she hit...her head on...the sink. Because she had blacked out." I said off the top of my head.

She looked skeptical but took out a form and began her interrogation.

"What class were you supposed to be in?"

"Transformation."

"So, what exactly happened?"

I didn't know what to say. I was pretty sure Sabrina's memory was still fuzzy.

"Well, I walked into the restroom, and once I finished, I washed my hands. I went to dry them off when I slipped on the wet floor. The next thing I remember is that I woke up and found Charlotte looking over me."

I stared at Sabrina in awe; she just winked at me as the nurse wrote everything down. Everyone seemed to be good at lying, *but* me. Which is pretty surprising. I guess stretching the truth doesn't come as naturally as thinking outside the box.

"Okay, then. I'm gonna run a few tests to make sure you're alright."

"I think you should check out Charlotte, too."

I stared at her. I told her I was fine, but I still felt pretty tired. I didn't want to worry, Sabrina, so I told the nurse I was okay. She checked Sabrina almost precisely as I had. Her temperature, pulse, and then asked one last question.

"Do you feel any pain, nausea, or dizziness?"

"My throat kind of hurts, and I have a slight headache."

"Okay. I know a spell. *Nemo plus doloris*!"

Before she could protest, she was eaten alive by a funnel of clouds. Naturally, these were fluffy, bright pink clouds with glitter bits in them. Probably to keep the patient calm, but most likely for little kids who were afraid of doctors.
The clouds kept spinning and spinning until they finally dispersed.

"Now you two can go to class," she waved her wand, and two nurse passes fluttered into our hands. We thanked her and headed back to class.

"Do you think it worked?" Sabrina asked me.

"We'll just have to wait and see."

"I hope it did. I've been waiting for this moment my entire life."

"That reminds me, you live on Earth, right?"

"Um, yeah...we can still be friends, right?"

"Of course! I was just gonna ask that since you're from Earth, why were you so surprised by Sam's watch?"

"Oh, yeah. I just figured that witches were too *good* for something as simple and boring as a watch. You know?"

I wanted to say not really, but I understood where she was coming from. She had probably looked up to witches and wizards her whole life. She must've thought we were so much better than humans, so she wanted to be one herself.

"Yeah. I get it."

"Remember, not a soul," she said as we got to the classroom, "I mean it. I don't want to risk losing any friends."

I nodded, even though I was confident that Sam and the twins wouldn't really care.

Then the voice in my head decided to speak. *You don't know them. They probably don't even like you. Why would they want to be friends with some human anyway?* I ignored it, and then I slowly and warily opened the classroom door. As soon as I did, the bell rang, and we had to avoid getting trampled.

"Girls! A word, please," the teacher called once we walked in. Sam and the twins watched and exchanged nervous glances as they silently exited the classroom.

"Have a seat, ladies."

We got our bags at sat at our desks in front of the room.

"Now tell me, girls, what on earth took you so long to use the facilities?"

"Sabrina slipped on some water and blacked out. We went and saw the nurse. We have passes," I held up my pass from the nurse for him to see.

He leaned forward and snatched the pass from my hand, inspecting it for any signs of forgery. Finally, he sighed.

"I'll have the janitor check the sinks for any leaks. Next time, be more careful. Alright?"

"Yes, sir," we both said.

"Now, your homework will be to turn your stone into a flower of your choice, and then to bring it back here tomorrow."

He handed us our stones, and we put them away.

"Okay. You are dismissed now…you can leave."

The teacher seemed a bit uncomfortable, so we left. Our friends were waiting for us when we left the room. Since great minds think alike, they all asked, "What happened?"

"What took you so long?"

"Are you guys, okay?"

"Sabrina, what was wrong with you in class?"

I wasn't sure how to answer the last question, but Sabrina and I did our best to answer them all.

"First of all, we took a long time because," Sabrina's eyes

reminded me of my promise. "…Because Sabrina fell in the rest-room."

She gave me a thankful look, "The floor was wet, and she slipped and hit her head on the sink."

Eliza's eyes went wide, and she grabbed Sabrina's head in her hands. "You poor thing! Are you okay? Should I cast a pain relief spell? Do you need some water?" she turned her head back and forth, frantically searching for any bruises.

"No, I'm fine. We went to the nurse, and she checked me out."

She looked at me gratefully, "Of course, Charlotte helped me the most. If she hadn't woken me up, I might still be uncon-scious on the floor!"

"Woah, Charlotte. Are you a doctor?" Alex beamed.

"I don't know about that. I just checked to see if she was alive. Splashed some water on her face. Nothing extraordinary."

"Sabrina seems to think otherwise," Sam said. Sabrina blushed.

"Well, now that you're all caught up, I think it's time we head to class," Eliza said.

We all got our things from our lockers and headed off to seventh period, Transportation, with Mr. Opoudipote. I swear these people are *trying* to have unpronounceable names.

CHAPTER 7

Alexander

When I saw Charlotte in first period, I was so excited to see her! I think I had every right to be. I mean, I had just discovered that probably the bravest witch *ever* was going to my school! *And* in my class!

In second period, I decided that I was going to be more like Charlotte. I was gonna think outside the box more, and be braver and more ambitious. I was gonna be everything Charlotte was, and more. We were gonna be the best of friends.

In third period, art, I decided to carve a picture frame. Did I decide I was making my frame for Charlotte? No. I just suddenly realized that my frame fit her picture. Did I actually see it? No. I just saw the paper she used. I knew the frame had to be elegant but original. Modern but unique. I got to work immediately and cast a concealing spell around my frame, so it would stay hidden. I didn't need anyone spoiling my surprise. Even when Charlotte wanted to see, I had to wait.

During lunch, I have to be honest. I *did* notice how impressed Charlotte was with Sam's spell, but I thought it was cool, too, so I figured no harm done. Still, I thought I shouldn't have soda unless Charlotte also did. But then she *insisted* that I had some. Charlotte was just so kind and selfless. I wished I was more like that.

In sixth period, I was ready to actually do some magic. We sat in our seats, the teacher started his introduction, and then Charlotte asked to use the restroom. She seemed kind of upset when she left, so I asked my sister if she thought Charlotte was alright.

"She seemed fine. I think she just didn't like the attention."

I quietly sighed a breath of relief. That's when I noticed the way Eliza was looking at me.

"What?" I demanded.

"It's just...now that I think of it, Charlotte didn't look too good."

I full-on panicked.

"What! Why didn't you say something sooner? What do you think is wrong? Can you go and check on her? Should we do something?"

I hadn't even realized that she had been laughing since my second question. It was a good thing that the teacher was busy in the back of the room, searching for rocks.

"I knew it!" she declared happily. I turned bright red and tore off my hat, which felt warm and pink in my hands. I stared at it, deep in thought. Eliza thinks I "love" Charlotte, even though I don't. What if Charlotte believes I love her?

My hat turned yellow. What if she thought so and started avoiding me! What if she didn't really want to be my friend at all!

My hat shocked me with a fearful static jolt.

"What now? Whatever you're thinking, you're over-thinking it."

I realized she was right. Sometimes, it was beneficial to have a twin sister. Then again, sometimes she's not so helpful...

I sighed. I wasn't really sure how I felt about Charlotte. I mean, I totally *adored* her, but do I *like* her? As a friend, absolutely. Anything more? I wasn't sure. Not that it mattered. I wasn't going to have any relationship plans anytime soon.

"Okay, class! Everyone, take the stones I passed out earlier." *When had he done that?* "Find the 'Transformation' chapter in your spellbooks, and turn your rocks into..." he paused either for dramatic effect or more time to decide, "...pillows!"

Everyone exchanged looks of confusion. We were going to turn rocks...into pillows. Wow. There isn't a turn-a-rock-into-a-pillow spell in our books, obviously.

"You will be writing the spell in groups of two. You must be next to each other to be partners. Of course, you may also work on your own."

Since Eliza sat next to Charlotte, who was in the facilities, and me, we had to work together. Sam and Sabrina were partnered up, and I noticed Eliza watching them. She had a neutral expression, but her hat was bright red. I tapped her shoulder.

"What?" she snapped.

"Your hat's burning."

She took it off, saw that it was red, and shoved it into her satchel.

"Stupid hat," she muttered.

"Sam seems to enjoy working with Sabrina." This wasn't true at all. In fact, Sabrina looked slightly uncomfortable, while Sam suggested what spells they should combine. Of course, my sister bought it.

"Well, maybe he'd enjoy working with me more if he just-" she cut herself off, realizing she'd fallen for her own trick.

"Touché."

Then Sabrina raised her hand, and she went to the restroom, leaving Sam on his own. He looked pretty disappointed, but not because of Sabrina. Because he would have to work on his own. I saw the way Eliza was watching Sam, who, begrudgingly, started the assignment.

"Go ahead. I've got this."

She looked back at me, smiled, then took off after her Romeo.

I was surprised that they got *anything* done, but I did see their rocks eventually turn into pillows. I, on the other hand, had no such luck. It took me a while to find a spell that even *made* pillows. Well, technically, it was considered "Head Cushions" in the book. Don't even ask why. Then I had to write the new spell, and by that time, the class was practically over. I kept on checking the door for Charlotte or even Sabrina, but nothing. They literally didn't come in until the bell rang.

Apparently, Sabrina slipped and blacked out. Charlotte was the one who kept her alive. I should've known that Charlotte knew first aid. I was looking forward to our last class because I was ready to show everyone what I'd made in art. I was pretty proud of it, and maybe it would confirm a long friendship between all of us.

Seventh period, Transportation. We walked in, and this time I sat next to Charlotte. The teacher's room seemed normal enough. He had his name written on the board and everything. All that was missing was the teacher himself. Then, right on cue, he appeared in the front of the classroom out of nowhere. One moment he wasn't there, and then with a flash of light, he was.

"Good afternoon, class. Welcome to your Transportation class. My name is Mr. Opoudipote, but you may call me Mr. O. In this class, you will be learning the basics of transportation from speed spells to teleportation."

I realized Charlotte didn't even *need* this class. After all, she had snuck to school completely undetected. I figured she ought to know, so I told her.

"You don't need this class. You're Ms. Speed-and-Stealth."

She really got a kick out of that. She could hardly suppress her laughter. But the teacher noticed and was not happy.

"You two," he pointed a finger at each of us, "Since you felt it was necessary to speak *now*, you may stay after class and continue your conversation with *me*."

Charlotte stopped laughing, and we both turned red. All eyes were on us, and neither of us liked it. I was too embarrassed even to muster an apology. Charlotte and I didn't speak the rest of the class period. To the point where I honestly began to fear that she was angry with me. But, we actually *did* speak when we were given our next assignment.

He told us that we had to change how fast a pencil fell to the ground by the end of class. He also said that we could work in partners...of our choice. He stared down Charlotte and me as he said it. We worked together in silence until I finally said something.

"Sorry I got you in trouble."

She looked up at me, seemingly surprised I'd spoken, and then laughed.

"You don't need to apologize. Did you think I was mad at you?"

This girl was freaking psychic.

"Um...maybe."

"Why would you think that? Is it because I haven't been talking to you? I haven't been talking because I don't want to get into any more trouble than I'm already in. Nothing else."

I felt a lot better about *that* situation, so now I figured we should *actually* get something done.

"Now that that's cleared up, we should probably get to work."

She nodded, and we completed the assignment. First, we had to find and combine the right spell, then we had to test it. When it didn't work, we had to try again, and again, and again. Eventually, we figured it out, tested it, and got the teacher's approval to talk among ourselves. Of course, he watched us suspiciously the whole time, but we mostly ignored him.

"So...it's been quite a day."

Charlotte laughed.

"Yeah, you could say that."

"It's been kinda strange. Especially the teachers."

"Don't even get me started on *them*," she joked.

"And is it just me, or are their names pretty weird?"

"I know, right? It's like they're in another language."

That gave me an idea.

"What if they *are* names in another language? Or maybe they're ancient names as old as Earth!"

Charlotte just stared at me, not saying anything. I sat back down but then realized Charlotte wasn't looking at me. She was looking straight ahead. I followed her gaze and saw her looking at Mr. Opoudipote. He had a hamburger in his hand, as well as a bag and drink from a fast-food restaurant. Then I realized that Charlotte was saying something.

"But, how?" she murmured. "He was...but he didn't..."

I snapped in front of her. "Charlotte?"

She blinked, "I was doing it again, wasn't I?"

I nodded.

"But the teacher. He was there for a second, I blinked, and then he was there with food. How?"

I realized what she meant. Mr. O never left the classroom, but he somehow managed to get a full meal without anyone noticing. Literally, in the blink of an eye. That was pretty strange, but we didn't have much time to dwell on it because the bell rang. The teacher suddenly appeared at the doorway.

"Okay, children. You won't be having a homework assignment from me. You are all dismissed," and he appeared back at his desk. Charlotte and I looked from him back to each other.

"Did he just..."

"Teleport? I think so," Sam said from behind us.

"Oh. *That's* what he was doing. I thought I was going crazy or something," Charlotte said in relief. "but...how'd he do that without a wand?"

We all began to leave when the teacher cleared his throat.

"Miss Parker. Mister Trevil. Stay here."

We exchanged looks as we went back to our seats.

"You two thought you could just walk away when I *specifically* told you two to stay?" he bellowed.

"It's not like that, sir!" Charlotte cried. "We just forgot!"

She sighed.

"I don't tend to have the best memory."

The teacher looked her up and down.

"Alright, then. Besides completely disregarding authority, do you know why you're here?"

"Because we were talking while you were?" We guessed.

"More like you decided that your petty conversation was more important than the direct instruction of your superiors!" He took a breath, "But more or less, you've got the right idea. Now, please do tell what your conversation was about." He crossed his legs and watched expectantly as Charlotte and I exchanged glances.

Finally, I stepped up. I told him, "I was complimenting her," as Charlotte watched with dismay. "I'm the one who spoke to her. She didn't respond. Charlotte shouldn't be in trouble. I should." That's when I knew Charlotte deserved my frame. I had gotten her in trouble for something that was my fault. Not only did I know that I needed to get her out of this mess, but I also knew I should give her my frame as an apology.

Charlotte looked astonished, while the teacher just nodded.

"Taking responsibility for your actions. Very good. Now, you are dismissed."

We both left the classroom and headed to homeroom in silence. After a few moments, Charlotte stopped and faced me.

"Thanks," she said with a smile.

"No problem."

She took my hand, "What would I do without a friend like you?"

I was too stunned to respond, but then she let go and said, "Come on, let's fill everyone in."

With no teachers around, she zipped through the hall as I just walked, lost in thought. I hadn't done anything special. I was just taking responsibility for my actions, just like the teacher said. Well, it clearly meant *something* to Charlotte, but I just felt that she shouldn't be punished for something that I did. Why did it mean *anything* to her?

By the time I got back to homeroom, it was practically empty. Charlotte had already filled everyone in, so I didn't have many questions to answer. Just one…from my sister.

"What took you so long? Charlotte got here ten minutes ago!"

"First of all, I'm pretty sure that is an exaggeration. Second of all, I was just thinking, and I took my time on the walk here."

She subtly nudged me and said, "What were you thinking about?"

I felt myself blush as Charlotte looked at me expectantly.

"Nothing, really. Just about...today."

Eliza studied me, "Right. Nothing else, huh?"

"Right," I said, eager to change the subject. "Now, why don't we get our art projects?"

"Oh, yeah! I forgot about those!" Sam said. With that, we left to get our things. Out in the hallway, we passed kids everywhere, some at their lockers, some standing around talking. It made me wonder where all of the teachers were, but since great minds think alike, Charlotte asked the question for me.

"Where are all of the teachers?" she asked.

"Mr. Blackwood said they had a meeting. They call kids' parents who've misbehaved. Even if it's something small."

I looked at Charlotte. She looked back at me. At that moment, we both knew that our parents would not be happy. I decided to reassure her.

"Hey, maybe you could show your parents your drawing? Might cheer them up, so you don't get in as much trouble."

"That reminds me, what did *you* make?"

I opened my locker and said, "Take a look."

She went to my locker and found the frame. She took it out and gasped.

"You did this?" she held up the frame for everyone to see, and everyone marveled at it. "It's beautiful!"

I blushed. It wasn't anything special. I'd carved a little bit of everyone into it. I'd overheard everybody's passions, so I used that info to make my frame. Each of the corners had something representing something about us. In the top right corner was a fancy teal painted masquerade mask with Eliza's name in the swirls. The bottom right corner had a stamped checkmark painted a metallic shade of magenta, and Sabrina's name painted silver. In the top left corner, I had a wand with Charlotte's name painted in a light, metallic shade of purple. Finally, in the bottom left was a carved drawing compass, but where a circle would be, 'Samuel' was carved.

Charlotte continued to gaze at my frame until she noticed something.

"Hey, Alex...?"

"Yes?"

"What about you? Nothing about *you* is on your own frame."

I shrugged, "There wasn't room, so I didn't worry about it. Besides, the frame isn't *for* me. It's for-"

"Wait. You didn't have *space*, so you didn't do anything about yourself?"

"Well, yeah. But also because-"

"I can fix that." She took her spellbook out of her belt. "Let's see..."

Her pages rapidly flipped as she searched for the right spell.

"Wait, what are you trying to do?"

She ignored me and kept looking for the spell. We all exchanged looks, trying to figure out what just happened. While Charlotte continued her search, Sam asked me, "Who is the frame for?"

I turned a little red, "Um...well... It's *supposed* to be for-"

"Yes! Got it!" We all turned our attention back to Charlotte.

"Now. Do you care to explain to us what you've 'got'?" Eliza asked.

"I found a spell that will give the frame more space! Then a bit of all of us will be on it!"

Before I could protest, she set down the frame, raised her wand, and said the words: "*Facere diutius!*"

I watched as clouds rapidly spun around the frame. It as like a tornado. Only, it was making the frame bigger. Once the swirling stopped, Charlotte began to waver.

"Woah! Charlotte?"

She steadied herself.

"Yeah? I'm fine. Just a little lightheaded."

Then, we all looked at the frame on the floor. It was no longer a long rectangle, but now a wide pentagon. Other than the point at the top being blank, the frame looked about the same.

"Now, you can finish it!"

"Well... I'm not sure...Besides, I've been trying to-"

"Well, let me do it for you!"

She set the frame back on the ground and began to search through her book once more.

"Stop!" I put my hand in her book, and she stopped searching to meet my eyes.

"What is it?"

"I've been trying to tell you. The frame is for you!"

She looked at me, mystified. "Really?"

"Yeah. It's for your drawing," I began to blush.

"Aw, that's so sweet," Eliza teased.

I turned bright red and shot Eliza a look.

"I have an idea! What if we hang up your drawing in the treehouse tomorrow?" Sabrina suggested.

"Good idea! We could put *all* our artwork there." Sam added.

They all took their art from their lockers and headed back to homeroom, leaving Charlotte and me behind. We both just looked at the nearly finished frame, wondering what to do with it.

"Alex."

"Yeah?"

"Is it okay if I...finish the frame?"

"Yeah. It's yours now."

She nodded and said, "*Plene perficere.*"

The clouds formed, but as they did, Charlotte started to quiver.

I caught her just before she fell.

"Are you okay?"

"I...think so. How's the frame?"

We both looked down, and at the top of the frame was a magician's hat and wand. My name was carved within the wand.

"It's perfect," we said together.

I picked up the frame and handed it to her. She smiled, and together we joined the others back in homeroom, a few minutes before the dismissal bell rang.

CHAPTER 8

Sabrina

Y ou have no idea how long I wanted someone to cast the "Magic Tongue" spell. Of course, I wish I went to the restroom first in my plan. When we had to do that assignment, I was partnered with Sam. I felt awful that I couldn't help. On top of that, *Richard* was sitting right behind me. I knew I couldn't cast a spell right to save my life. At least, not *yet*, I couldn't. Who knows what would happen if I tried?

The worst part was that I had to wait for the perfect moment to go to Charlotte. If I went too soon, the teacher would know something was up. If I went too late, he might begin to wonder where Charlotte was. Finally, after about five minutes, I decided to go for it, and I did. I couldn't wait to show Grandma!

Then, we all finally got to see what Alex made, and he gave it to Charlotte! I thought that was pretty sweet of him. When they got back, the frame had a magician's hat and wand on it.

"Wow, you guys, it's perfect! Even better than before," I looked at Alex, "No offense."

"None taken. Besides, Charlotte finished it."

She shrugged. "What can I say? It wasn't complete without all of us, part of it."

Everyone nodded in agreement. When the dismissal bell rang, we all stood up to leave.

"Well, see you guys tomorrow," Sam said as he walked out the door. We all said our goodbyes and headed to the school's entrance. Charlotte, Eliza, and Alex all got on the same bus. Surprisingly none of them seemed to see each other. Then all of the buses took off, leaving me, Sam, and many other students. I walked over to Sam and asked him what all these other kids were doing.

Then, the kids started disappearing. Some in a flash of light, some in a swirl of leaves, some even engulfed in flames.

"What's going on?"

"What do you mean? They're going home. I have to go too." He took a step away from me and raised his wand.

"You sound pretty new to all this," he lowered his wand, "Where are you from?"

I hesitated, "Um...Earth?"

"Oh, that makes sense. Well, let me show you the ropes. If you live on Earth or you don't have a bus stop, so you can either send yourself home or wait for your parents. Most of us, like yours truly, just take themselves home."

He raised his wand again. "I've got to go, but you can always just take yourself home, ya know. *Mitte in domum suam!*"

Then I watched as he was engulfed by a column of fire. I gasped and staggered backward. Naturally, I ran into the famous clumsy-kid-catcher, Richard.

"You've been falling for me a lot lately."

I turned bright red, "Sorry about that, ...again."

"It's alright." He helped me to my feet, "I don't mind."

I rubbed the back of my neck, "Thanks for, you know, catching me all day. I'll try not to be so clumsy."

He nodded. "Well, I should be leaving." He took a step away from me and smiled, "See ya, Sabrina."

Instead of anything startling, he simply melted into the ground. No words were necessary. He just melted into his own shadow, and then *that* slowly faded away. I sighed and realized that this was my chance to test out Charlotte's spell. I took a deep breath and slowly said a spell to take me home aloud. At first, nothing happened, but suddenly everything went white. I opened my eyes and found myself in my room at Grandma's house. I sat up and realized I was completely drained of my energy. I struggled to drag myself out of bed, sort of like a typical school morning, and groggily followed my Grandma's humming. When I walked in, Grandma was stirring something in her cauldron. She heard me walk in and smiled.

"Good! You're awake. I was just fixing you some tea."

"In the cauldron?"

"Well, it is technically a potion, but it tastes just like tea!"

She poured some into a small teacup. I shrugged and took a sip. It was pretty good, and suddenly I felt full of energy.

"That should keep you awake until dinner," she smiled.

"What happened?"

"You cast your first spell! That's what happened!"

"But...what happened *after* that? I remember casting the spell, but not going to bed. And why am I so tired?"

Grandma gave me a warm smile and said, "Patience. You need your energy. But for now, you should get started on your homework. Dinner will be ready soon enough."

"But, I thought I was helping with dinner. Just like every night."

"Nonsense. Just half an hour ago, you had passed out from exhaustion. You need your tea, some rest, and to do your homework. Now go on!"

Before I could protest, I was whisked away back into my room. I hated it when Grandma did that.

With a sigh, I got started on my homework. I picked out a book for tomorrow, wrote my paragraph for why, and then got started on my first spell casting assignment. It was a lot harder than I expected, so I put it off for later, leaving me with only the survey. I began to fill it out when I remembered that I was supposed to call everyone. I dashed through the hall at lightning speeds back into the kitchen.

That was when I realized how fast I had run. I stared at my feet and slowly began giggling. Soon I doubled over, breaking into a fit of laughter without a hint of fatigue in my body. Grandma rushed to my side with a teacup in her hands, seemingly worried. I stopped laughing to catch my breath as Grandma urged me to drink more "tea." I pushed it away and got back on my feet. I took a deep breath and slowly began to giggle again. I was pretty sure Grandma was trying to tell me something, but I was too busy laughing.

Finally, I stopped to meet my Grandmother's worry-filled eyes.

"What's wrong?" I asked her.

"I thought you were going crazy!"

"I'm fine. Just a bit of an adrenaline rush!"

I was suddenly excited and jumpy. Ready to run again. I began hopping from foot to foot, suddenly anxious to take off.

"Grandma, can I go run outside? Please?"

She examined me, inspecting whether I was myself or an insane imposter.

"Why?"

I began to run in place, "I don't know. Maybe because I might have super speed?"

Grandma rolled her eyes. "Oh, really? Then run five laps around the house. I'll time you."

I waited for her to get a stopwatch. Of course, she didn't. Instead, she said, "I'll keep count for you."

I shrugged and stepped outside, got in a ready position, and waited for Grandma to get over the fact that I was serious. Once she did, she counted me off, "On your mark, ...get set..." She brought up her hand, and the millisecond it went back down, I took off. Those five laps were nothing. Took me about... what, three seconds? I casually went back inside to see the look on my Grandmother's face.

She looked in her cauldron and asked, "What on Earth was in that tea?"

I laughed. "I don't know, but I think that's what happens when you make tea in a cauldron."

She gave me a serious look and warily took a sip of tea. To

test this new theory, she ran off to her room. When she got back, it was clear the tea hadn't given her any new powers. But, if that wasn't how I got them, then where did I get them from?

I zipped back into my room and got my teacup. This time, when I put the cup to my lips, I felt a small static shock. It didn't hurt or anything, so I drank the rest. It filled me with more energy, and I ran back into the kitchen.

"Grandma?" I said, startling her and making her drop her ladle into the bubbling tea. "Whoops."

She turned to me, "Yes, dear?"

"The tea...What kind is it?"

"It's *supposed* to be an energy potion. I added in some Black and Yerba Mate tea leaves."

I gave her my I-need-an-explanation look.

"They were specifically said to help replenish energy, increase endurance, and even stimulate the senses."

Before I could go any deeper into thought, I remembered why I had come into the kitchen in the first place.

"Grandma, where's your crystal ball?"

"In the office. What do you need it for? You need to get back to your homework, remember?"

"Yes, ma'am. I remember, but I need to call my classmates. We're doing a survey, and we need to do it together."

Grandma shrugged, "I know where to find you. Go on."

I took off into the "office," which was really just the basement. I guess since she "worked" down there at a desk, she liked to call it her office. All she really did was find sorcerers on quests, and point them in the right direction. She used the elements of nature to either help them solve puzzles, guide them on their journeys, or even help them fight enemies.

On her desk was her crystal ball. I shut my eyes and waved my hands over it. Concentrating. Then I spoke a chant that I had made up on the spot, using the tricks that Grandma had taught me.

"Crystal ball. Crystal ball. I have some friends that you must call. Alex and Eliza, Charlotte and Sam. I need them all.

The whole...clan."

I couldn't think of anything that rhymed with Sam.

"Once called, the last thing I need is for you to project the whole live feed."

I opened my eyes, and the ball was glowing bright green. I looked into the large mirror hanging on the wall in front of Grandma's desk. Three sections of the mirror were filled with static. Then the largest one cleared, revealing Alex and Eliza side by side.

"Hey, guys!"

They both looked confused, "Where are you? We can't see anything," Eliza said.

"Oh! Hold on."

I rushed behind the desk and sat in front of the ball. I put my hands over it and then quickly pulled them away, like peek-a-boo. Another trick Grandma taught me. If I did it again, they wouldn't see me, just like before.

"Okay, *now* we see you."

"What'd I miss?" Sam said.

"Guys, you should probably project the feed onto something," I suggested.

"One step ahead of you," the twins said at the same time. I suppressed a laugh. Great minds *do* think alike.

"On it," Sam said.

Then, I looked in the mirror and noticed the third section was still filled with static.

I muted myself and asked the crystal ball to call Charlotte again. It did, but nothing happened. Maybe she didn't have a crystal ball. I went back online with my friends.

"Has anyone heard from Charlotte?" I asked.

Everyone shook their heads.

"Well, we'll see her tomorrow. We can do the survey with her in the morning. Everyone has them?"

They all held them up for me to see.

"Good. Now let's get started!"

We filled out the survey in no time. We all made sure that

we had the same answers to ensure that we were put in a group together.

"Bye, guys! Don't forget to see if you guys can come to my house tomorrow!"

"We won't!" They all said at once. Then the mirror went blank and showed me, sitting at Grandma's desk. I smiled at my reflection and zipped up to my room.

I took the book I'd packed for school and started reading it. I learned about five of the elements of nature. They were some of the most potent magical elements a sorcerer could possess. They were the elements of water, flora, air, fire, and electricity. Every one thousand years, a group of children from magical lineage was said to discover these elements' magic within themselves. They gave them unique powers that would help them defend the world from evil when the time was right.

I couldn't help but wonder if I had been one of those children. What if I had one of the elements, and it was up to me to find the other children? I pushed that thought out of my mind and kept reading.

These children's powers were first stimulated when their enemies had found them and identified them successfully.

Uh-oh. Now I was hooked on the idea that I was one of these kids. If I was, that could mean I was in grave danger. Panicked, I ran back to the kitchen to find Grandma.

Once I did, though, my super-speed took over my speech. What I said was, "Grandma! I was reading one of your books on magic, and one of them said something about superpowers and kids getting them when their enemies had found them, so I think I might be in danger if I'm one of those kids! Plus, it would explain how I was suddenly getting superpowers now that I'm a real witch and stuff, but I hardly think I could defend myself from evil or anything. I mean, all I can do is run fast. Now, if I had telekinesis or something, *that* would be another story. Even still, I'm not sure if I could protect myself. Plus, that means there are other kids out there that we have to find-" then my grandma put her finger to my lips, and I stopped talking.

"Those new 'powers' of yours have you talking a mile a minute. Now. Ask me *one* question to summarize whatever you just said."

I thought about my question carefully, took a deep breath, and slowly asked my grandmother, "Do I have elemental magic?"

CHAPTER 9

Elizabeth

Wasn't it sweet of Alex to give Charlotte that apology frame? I sure thought so. Plus, I think Charlotte liked it! Honestly, it was kind of hard to tell. I mean, it seemed that way at first, but then she insisted that it was improved. Well, she *did* want to make sure Alex was a part of it, so I assume that was good. Of course, the two love birds stayed behind for a while. I'd rather not make any assumptions, but I'm sure nothing terrible happened. Otherwise, I'm sure Alex's hat would have said something. It was a rainbow of mixed emotions when he got back, and Charlotte's hat was glowing with excitement.

Once the bell rang, we packed our things and headed out. Alex and I found our weird bus driver and got on. Alex got the window seat, so I sat closest to the isle. I heard the bus driver talking to a student in the front. When I peeked over, I saw familiar curly hair. I stood up and walked to the front.

"Charlotte?"

She and the bus driver turned their attention to me.

"Eliza! This is your bus?"

"You know this girl?" the driver asked me.

I nodded, "Yes, sir. In fact, she's on our bus. She just missed it this morning."

The driver turned his attention back to Charlotte.

"Alright. Now try not to miss the bus again."

Charlotte nodded, and I led her back to Alex and my seats. You should've seen the look on his face when he saw Charlotte! It was priceless!

"Charlotte! What are you doing here?"

"Turns out, this is my bus too!" She looked between Alex and me, "Um...can I sit with you guys?"

"Of course!" I grabbed my things out of Alex's seat, "You can sit by Alex!" Charlotte happily plopped down beside Alex, who looked more confused than a puppy in a mirror. I sat in the seat in front of them and turned to face them.

"So, Charlotte. How do you like Alex's *gift*?"

Alex gave me a death stare, but Charlotte just smiled, "It's beautiful! I can't wait to hang it in the treehouse but to think he nearly didn't put *himself* in it. I'm glad I did it for him. It just wasn't complete, ya know?"

I nodded, and all the while, Alex blushed furiously.

"Do you know what stop you are?"

"Um...I think I'm about two stops *before* you in the mornings, so I'm probably two stops *after* you in the afternoons."

Just then, the bus came to a stop, and I nearly fell out of my seat. I looked out the window and saw that we were home already. I got my bags together, "Bye, Charlotte! C'mon, Alex."

Charlotte got out of the seat and let Alex by. Then we got off and took our brooms out of our handbags. With one last wave to Charlotte, the bus left. We flew across the street to our house, and as we did, I couldn't help but tease my brother on our way inside.

"Alex and Charlotte sitting in a tree!" I chanted on our way towards the door. I know it was childish, but we were all thinking about it.

"Oh, yeah?" Alex said when we walked in. He cupped his hands over his mouth and shouted, "Eliza and Sam sittin in a-" before I quickly covered his mouth in case mom and dad were home.

"Okay! Would you shut up? If mom and dad are here, I will mute you."

In case you don't know what that means, muting is when you cast a spell that takes away a person's voice, and then you store that person's voice in a jar until you feel merciful. Or you could smash the jar leaving them voiceless forever.

"And I'm smashing the jar."

Then we looked at each other and burst into a fit of laughter. Man, I love my brother. "Come on, let's do our homework."

We went upstairs and heard someone crying.

"Hello?"

The crying stopped, and then a small voice said, "Eliza?"

I went into Alex's shared room to find a five-year-old in tears with a half-dead plant in his lap.

"Oh, no, Josh. What happened?"

My little brother ran up to me and grabbed my legs.

It's Snappy! I was supposed to look after him for the week, but-but-" He burst back into tears.

I sat down and cradled him in my lap. Of course, you'd trust a five-year-old with a venus fly trap. It probably hadn't been home for more than ten minutes, and it was already dying. Alex went to the plant, picked up the pot, and examined it. Then he gently touched one of the brown dying leaves. Before I could scold him for crumbling it, the leaf turned green again, full of life.

"Alex...what did you do?"

He gasped and nearly dropped it. He looked at his hand.

"I...I don't know."

Joshua loved it.

"Alex! Do it again! Do it again!"

Alex sat down and rested the pot in his lap. He closed his eyes and laid his hands on Snappy. Almost instantly, the plant grew a foot taller.

"Alex, what are you *doing*?"

He opened his eyes and jumped.

"I did that?!"

Joshua clapped excitedly.

"Alex! Can you make me bigger too? I wanna be big too!"

Alex examined his hands.

"I think it only works on plants," Alex told him.

"Awww. I wish *I* was a plant."

"Josh, Alex, and I have homework to do, so if you'll excuse us," I said, ushering Alex out of the room.

Once we got to my room, I calmly shut the door and took a deep breath. "Alex…what…did you do…to that plant?"

He shrugged.

I took another breath.

"Try it on something else. That's not a plant."

He looked around and then picked up a pen. He closed his eyes, pen in his hand. After a few seconds of silent tension, nothing happened. Then Alex slowly opened his eyes.

"I guess it only works on plants," he said calmly.

How in the world was he being so calm!?

"Okay, then. Let's just start on our homework."

He gave me a confused look, then examined his hands again. Then he pinched his left wrist and flinched with pain. I put my hands on my hips.

"No, Alex. This *isn't* a dream."

He looked from me to his hands before finally saying, "Awesome."

I rolled my eyes and got started without him. Maybe about half an hour later, a loud voice called out to Alex and me. Without hesitation, we raced downstairs. I made a dash for the living room. As usual, I got to the crystal ball first, and my slow-poke brother staggered behind. That might have been because the house was a mess, and all of Josh's toys were everywhere. Surprisingly I was able to avoid them all gracefully. I guess I just went with the flow.

Anyways, I got to the ball and quickly said the dumb rhyme.

"Crystal ball, crystal ball. We are here, answer the call."

I don't know why you have to say a rhyme, 'cause if you

ask me, it's just a waste of time. We heard Sabrina, but we didn't see her, which was strange because that's how crystal balls work. You're supposed to *see* the person you're talking to. Anyway, long story short, we finished the survey without Charlotte. Poor Alex waited for her to call back, but she never did. I honestly felt bad. He seemed to look up to Charlotte, so I tried to comfort him.

"Hey, remember, Charlotte still has a roof to fix. Besides, we'll see her tomorrow." He smiled, and we finished the rest of our homework in the living room. About half an hour after we were done, our big sister Jordan got home. As usual, she went straight to our bedroom and got started on homework. She doesn't like to waste time. As she always says: the sooner you start, the sooner you finish.

It hadn't been over five minutes before we heard a loud boom come from upstairs. Alex sighed, and I rolled my eyes.

"I've got it."

I went upstairs to find an enormous green cloud of smoke flooding our room, and making its way to Joshua's. I quickly shut his door and raced for my bedroom. I squinted to see through the smoke, and I tried to hold my breath. Who knew if this stuff was poisonous? I got to my room and saw Jordan coughing with her shirt covering her mouth and ineffectively fanning the smoke away from her. Then I saw the source. Our cauldron was on fire. This must've been the third time this month that Jordan had messed something up while rushing through a spell.

Instinctively, I thrust my hands towards it, and a jet stream of water shot out. The stream kept going and going until the cauldron stopped smoking. Once it did, I looked at my hands, took a deep breath, and fainted.

Not sure how long I was out, but all I know is that when I woke up, I was chewing something. I slowly sat up, and Jordan and Alex were at my sides. Jordan was on my left, white as a ghost, and Alex was on my right, leaning against my bed on the floor, eyes nearly shut.

"Are you okay, Alex?"

He looked up at me and smiled weakly.

"I'm fine. Are you okay?"

"Yeah... I'm not entirely sure what happened, though..."

I gave him a look, implying that I wanted an explanation, but he was fast asleep, so I looked at Jordan. She sighed.

"You...put out the cauldron, but...you didn't have your wand. And then Alex...he came in and saw you on the floor. He asked for Maca..."

"Huh?"

"It's a plant. It enhances energy and reduces fatigue. How he knew that I don't know..."

I realized I was still chewing, and I spat the Maca out in the trash.

"So, I was eating some kind of *mystery plant*?"

"Yeah, but that's the thing. I don't *have* any."

"What? Then where did he get them?"

"He...I think he grew them. I watched him close his eyes and cup his hands, and suddenly there was diced Maca...but he didn't have his wand either..."

I wondered if I was still unconscious and dreaming. Maybe I'd inhaled some of the smoke. I pinched myself and sighed.

"What is *happening* today?!" I practically yelled, waking up Alex with a jolt.

"Come on, Alex." I got up and helped him to his feet. "Go take a nap in *your* room." He rubbed his eyes groggily, and I helped him get to his room. Joshua was on the floor, talking to Snappy. He looked up when we walked in and saw Alex.

"Is he okay?"

I nodded. "Alex's just tired."

I tucked him in his bed like I did with Josh and left. I went back to my room and flopped back onto my bed. I wasn't sure what to even think about. My water hands? Alex's plant powers? Charlotte's roof? Sam? I didn't even know!

I groaned as loud as I could into my pillow and made my

sister look up from her potion-making.

"Are you okay?"

I wasn't sure how to answer, so I didn't, and she didn't pry me.

"If you're gonna sulk, keep doing what you're going. But if you want to *talk*...well, you're definitely not doing it right."

That's my sister for you. A real comedian.

I rolled over onto my back and concentrated on a circular shape on the ceiling. I just started to space out when I heard my name. I sat up, "Huh?" Then I was splashed with water.

"What the? What was *that* for?" I demanded.

Jordan stared at me in disbelief.

"I didn't do that. *You* did."

"How could *I* have done that?"

"I don't know. You tell me."

I thought about it. I have water hands, so maybe I did do this myself. Then I realized I wasn't wet. Not even a little bit. Cross-legged in my bed, I began to meditate. I pictured myself surrounded by water bubbles. I heard a muffled voice call to me, but I ignored it. Now I made them spin around me. Faster and faster until they formed a protective ring around me.

I slowly and calmly opened my eyes. The bubbles kept spinning, and I kept concentrating. I made them stop, and I reached out to touch one. As soon as I did, and all of the other bubbles popped and splashed me with water. I just laughed. I had always loved popping bubbles when I was little.

Then I noticed that not only was I dry but my bed was too. I decided to try the bubbles again. This time, I kept my eyes open and formed a small water bubble in my hands. I tossed it up in the air and caught it without popping it. I played with it for a while. Bouncing it off the wall, balancing it on my head, until I decided to check on Alex. I squeezed the bubble in my hand, and it popped.

I went to Alex's room and found his side of the room covered in vines. I looked on Josh's side and found them both staring at the vines in amazement. I looked at Alex.

"Did you do this?"

He shrugged, and I sighed.

"Yes, you did. Come on. Clean 'em up," I said, clapping my hands.

He took a breath, closed his eyes, and held his hands out towards them. They slowly retracted back to his hands, being absorbed into his palms. I honestly wasn't sure whether it was cool or nauseating.

Once they were all gone, he opened his eyes and gasped at the now perfectly clean wall. He looked at me.

"What is happening to me?"

"I don't know, but whatever it is," I made a water bubble and spun it on my finger, "we need to get to the *bubble* of it."

He cracked a smile, and I began to giggle.

"Grab your things, I want to see what you can do."

Once he came downstairs, I flew out the door on my broom with my satchel slung across my shoulder. It felt good, the wind whipping through my hair. I circled the house until Alex decided to join me.

"Where are we going?" He called to me as we flew down our "street".

"Just follow me," I told him, and I dove down to Earth. Once I broke through the clouds, I found myself increasing speed. I tried not to fly too low to the ground so I wouldn't be spotted, but it only a couple of minutes before I found myself flying just barely above a forest of evergreens.

"Perfect," I said, once I'd found a branch big enough to land on. I slowed down and hovered above it. Then, I slowly and carefully got off of my broom, and...

"Hey," Alex said out of nowhere.

"Gah!" I stumbled backward off of the branch and began falling. I turned around as branches whizzed past my face. I saw the ground getting closer and closer by the millisecond. Time seemed to slow down as I covered my eyes with my hands, bracing for impact when, at the last second, I felt something grab my ankle. I suddenly jerked upward and began to sway. I looked up to see a long vine wrapped around my left ankle. I saw Alex at the top holding on. I smiled, put my fingers to my lips, and whistled sharply. My broom flew straight to me, and when I say *straight*, I mean straight to my *head*.

It came too quickly for me to move anything except my hands in front of my face. I braced for impact, again, only this time it passed right through me. You read that right. My broom went through me and hovered directly below where I was dangling, suddenly dripping with water. I gasped and slowly reached out to grab it. When my hand didn't phase through it, I clutched the wet broomstick and let my ankle gradually phase through the vine. I plopped onto my broom, steadied myself, and flew back up to my brother.

My poor brother was white as snow, and I rested my hand on his shoulder.

"Thanks."

He sighed, "No problem."

"How did you do that? I mean, you came out of nowhere. I thought you lost me."

"I did, but...then I saw you, clear as day. Maybe it has something to do with the trees? Since I have plant powers and all."

I shrugged and remembered why we came.

"So, I brought you here so we could see what we can do. I can do this."

I made a giant water bubble in my hands. Then tossed it in the air and let it splash onto my head while staying completely dry.

"Apparently I can also phase through things. Like, when my broom came to me, it went straight at my head. And I made my ankle phase through your vines."

I demonstrated by holding up my hand, turning it to mist, then solidifying it again. Something I hadn't known I could do before then.

"Now, what can *you* do so far?"

He looked down at his palms.

"Um...I can grow supposedly any plant from my hands, and I *might* be able to find anything in a forest, but I don't think that counts."

"Can you shoot leaves?"

He shrugged and then thrust his palm out towards a tree. Suddenly, every needle on the evergreen we shot through the forest until they were out of view.

We looked at each other and simply said, "Nice."

"Too bad you can't phase through things too," I said.

He shrugged, but then I got another idea.

"Maybe you can phase through trees!"

He carefully walked across the branch and touched the bark at the center of the tree. Instead of phasing through it, vines erupted from the tree and began to wrap themselves around our branch. Instinctively, we hopped onto our brooms and watched as the vines engulfed only the branch we'd been standing on.

Curiously, I hopped off of my broom onto the vine-covered branch. It was now a lot sturdier, and I jumped on it experimentally.

"So, it looks like you can add strength to plants too. Just like you did with Snappy."

He nodded, and I hopped back onto my broom.

"C'mon. Let's put our new powers to the test."

We went to an abandoned school ground I'd passed on our way to the forest. We went to their deserted football field, and I explained the plan to my brother.

"So, I think we should have a little...battle against each other. Using our powers, and not anything else."

He just nodded and smiled at the challenge. We are a very competitive family, so I knew a battle was going to be fun.

"Ladies first," Alex called from the other end of the field.

"Fine."

I summoned an enormous water bubble and hurled at Alex. Instead of dodging, he threw his hand upwards, and a long line of tall leaves shielded him as the bubble burst against them.

He laughed and sent a fleet of razor-sharp leaves my way. At first, I was startled, but then I remembered. Nothing phases me. I just needed to keep misting forward, and that's precisely what I did. I let myself dissolve as the leaves whizzed by. One leaf nearly struck my arm, but I let it phase right through. Alex's attack left me scratchless.

Taken aback, I watched as Alex tried to come up with a new game plan. I just kept walking forward without a care in the world, until he raised his arms and threw them towards me. Then I noticed what was in his hands. Vines. They whipped and lashed at me, and I gracefully dodged them. Leaping and ducking, Alex could only lay a single leaf on me.

Of course, since my brother's strong suit is nature, leaving that leaf on me wasn't such a good idea. I hadn't realized it until it was too late, and suddenly the long fuzzy vines sprouted from that leaf that suspended me in the air. Before I could phase through them, they began to tickle me. I was being attacked by a tickle monster, and it was awful. I laughed so hard I could hardly breathe, and my brother finally called out, "Do you yield?"

I wanted nothing more than to continue our fight...but I also just had to stop the tickling. Between gasps for breath, I managed to wheeze, "Yes! I surrender!"

Call me whatever you want, but when you get tickled by fuzzy vines, I want you to tell me how long you lasted. Let me go, and I slowly caught my breath. Then I called out, "We should head back. Mom and dad should be home by now."

We summoned our brooms and sped off back home. The sun had set, and I could only hope that our parents hadn't been home for too long. Once we got to the door, I leaned in close to the door and listened for them. I heard clanging of pots being pulled from our cabinets, so I knew that they had just gotten home.

"Dad's in the office on the phone," Alex suddenly said.

"How do you..." I paused and realized Alex could see through the wood in the house. He must've been able to see through natural materials, which would explain how he found me in the forest. I asked him where mom was. He looked to the left and then said, "In the kitchen getting dinner ready. Josh and Jordan are both upstairs, so we can go in."

I nodded. Then Alex took a breath and misted underneath the door. There was just enough space for me to squeeze my mist-self through. I solidified on the other side and quickly and quietly dashed up the stairs. Out of the corner of my eye, I swear I saw Alex walk straight through the door while keeping it closed. I was definitely going to ask him about that, but first, I needed to stay out of trouble with my parents. I got to my room and waited for Alex to join me. Once he came upstairs, I asked him about it. He just shrugged, and I mentally added 'walking through wood' to Alex's list of powers.

Anyways, we went back to our rooms and acted like nothing happened. I was playing with bubbles when I heard my mom call us down for dinner. I popped them and raced downstairs. Everyone got to the dinner table, and my mom had already set our plates at our seats. So, we dug in. Of course, like *sane* people, but we were all pretty hungry. My parents took a seat at each end of the table. After a few moments of silence, my dad cleared his throat.

"So, how were your first days of school?"

We all gave him the same answer, "Good."

Except for Joshua, "Awesome! Guess what happened today?"

"What happened?"

"Snappy's leaves fell off and turned brown, and then Alex made him grow bigger! Plus, his leaves are all better now!" Our parents both turned to Alex expectantly, and he just shrugged, grabbing at the back of his neck.

"Josh's plant was...well...it needed some growing help, so I...um...used some magic on it."

My parents didn't seem to think much of it, so we continued our dinner. Jordan told us about her Chemistry class on Earth, and how it's just like potion-making. Alex and I just talked about our new friends: Charlotte, Sam, and Sabrina. Then we asked if we could go to Sabrina's house every day after school.

"Well...where does she live?" We paused.

"On Earth," we said at once.

My parents exchanged a nervous look.

"Don't worry! They don't know anything about us! I'm sure if they don't, their neighbors won't either. Besides, we can always..." I hesitated. Erasing memories usually gets complicated and is pretty risky, so I decided not to suggest it. "We could...come...right back! Yeah! We have the spell memorized!"

After a few moments of silent tension, our parents sighed, and mom said,

"As long as you're home in time for dinner. Which will be at sunset from now on."

CHAPTER 10

Samuel

I got home and did my homework. Once I finished, since no-body was home, I cleaned up around the house. Being an only child, I didn't have anything better to do. After cleaning up, I went outside on the roof and just enjoyed the sunlight. I found myself naming cloud shapes until I fell asleep.

I dreamt I was on Charlotte's roof, and it looked the same as it had in my last dream, except for the boulder. It was missing and in its place was an enormous hole. Charlotte was looking into it and seemed to be talking to someone. She leaned closer over it, still talking, then tried to take a step back. Instead of staying on the roof, she slipped back towards the hole.

"Charlotte!" I called out to her.

But instead of helping her in any way, I just made her jump with surprise into the hole. I dove in after her, only to find her hovering over her bed. Before I could process what was happening, I found my face buried into Charlotte's mattress.

"Sam?" I thought I heard Charlotte say. I was pretty sure I heard two gasps from other people, but I wasn't sure, so I sat up and rubbed my head. I saw that I was in Charlotte's room with her and who I could only assume were her older siblings. I wasn't sure how I'd know what Charlotte's room looked like in a dream or if she had siblings, and then I realized I wasn't dreaming. The slight headache proved it.

"Um…hey, Charlotte."

"What are you doing here? How do you even know where I live?"

I shrugged. "One minute, I'm on my roof cloud gazing. The next, I'm on your roof, watching you fall into a hole."

That's when I realized Charlotte was flying *without* a broom.

"How are you doing that?"

"Doing what?"

"Um…*flying*."

As though she hadn't noticed, she looked down at the ground. Once she saw that she was, in fact, flying, she gasped and dropped suddenly.

"Are you okay?" I asked, helping her up.

"Yeah, but I'm not sure how I did that either."

"Try it again," I encouraged. "Maybe you can control it."

So she did. She took a breath and hopped into the air. Instead of coming back down, she stayed in the air and squealed with excitement.

"I can *fly*!" Just to be sure, she pinched herself. Once confirmed that it was legit, she flew back out of the hole in her roof and peeked in at me.

"Care to join?" she asked.

"I don't know. Care to help me up?"

She laughed and flew back to me.

"Maybe you have powers too! You try to fly."

I was doubtful but tried anyway. I closed my eyes and jumped into the air. Let's just say I didn't fly. Instead, just before my rear made contact with the floor, I found myself…no longer myself. I was a cloud of smoke instead. I'm not sure how I could, but I heard Charlotte gasp.

Being a cloud of smoke, I felt weightless. Free. It's hard to keep from dispersing, though. Eventually, I gave up and let myself solidify again, just in time for my butt to hit the ground with a *thud.*

"Sam! Where did you go?"

"Nowhere. I was the smoke cloud."

Charlotte started to say something but changed her mind.

"So…care to explain the hole in your roof?"

She motioned for me to follow her as she flew back through the hole. I turned back into the smoke and followed her, the best I could. Luckily, she brought a gust of wind behind her when she flew, so staying with her was a breeze. She'd sat on the edge of the roof, feet dangling over the edge. I solidified next to her, looking at the clouds and endless buildings of our civilization.

"So, I was in my room working on homework. I'd completely forgotten about the boulder when I suddenly heard cracking above me. It turns out, my siblings had forgotten about my advice that morning and were trying to lift it with their magic. Only, instead of using an anti-gravitational spell, they tried to use a kind of telekinetic spell, that used their own strength instead of their minds."

She paused to make sure I was still listening, and I nodded for her to continue.

"Which is equivalent to them picking it up themselves. As you can see," Charlotte motioned towards the hole, "that didn't work out too well. I looked up, just as the boulder broke through my roof directly above me. It happened so fast I could hardly react. I just put my hands up, as though I could've caught it. I didn't, but…I somehow kept it from crushing me."

I just stared at her, mystified, and ready for her to continue.

"I heard my siblings call for me, and since I heard them, I knew I hadn't been crushed. I slowly opened my eyes and saw the boulder, hovering above my hands. I realized I was somehow holding it up and rapidly losing energy. I wasn't sure what to do, so I squeezed my hands into fists and punched the rock without touching it. It exploded, and then…I blacked out."

Charlotte saw the worried expression on my face and reassured me.

"Don't worry. I'm fine. I don't think I was out for longer than ten minutes. I remember waking up to my siblings, cleaning up the debris in my room."

She sighed and looked down, as though trying to see through the clouds. I looked down too and caught a glimpse of what looked like a flock of geese passing under us.

"Sam…" Charlotte said, still looking down.

I looked up, "Yeah?"

"How did you get here?" She asked, meeting my eyes.

"I…I'm not sure. I thought I was dreaming I was here. Just like last night-" Charlotte looked confused, but I wasn't sure how to explain.

"So…you've come to my house before?"

"I mean…I don't think a dream counts, so…no?"

"Well, you thought you were dreaming earlier, but you're here now, right?"

I thought about that. So, my dreams aren't really dreams? I was confused.

"Alright, then." I stood up, "I'm gonna get back home. My parents should be back soon."

I helped her to her feet. "I'll see you tomorrow."

She smiled, "See you tomorrow." Charlotte turned and hopped back through the gaping hole in her roof, and I woke up on mine.

Trust me, I was as confused as you are.

There was no way that was a dream, right?

I jumped off my roof and raced inside to find the family's crystal ball. I immediately called Charlotte. At first, there was just static, but it wasn't long before she answered.

"Sam? Is everything alright?"

"I'm fine…just checking something." I took a breath and asked her if I had been to her house before.

"What are you talking about? You just left…right? You're not still on my roof, are you?"

"No, I'm here. I just…woke up? I'm not really sure. It felt like I just woke up, so I was checking to see if it was a dream. All

I needed was a confirmation, so thanks. See you tomorrow."

With that, I hung up and tried to make sense of what had just happened. I did go to Charlotte's house, but I didn't leave my roof. Eventually, I gave up trying and waited for my parents to get home.

I was lying on my bed, staring at the ceiling when I felt something tickle my nose. I rubbed it, but the feeling stayed. It got stronger until I finally sneezed, loud and hard. I rubbed my nose again and looked up to find the edge of my bed was on fire.

"What the?!"

Without thinking, I scooped up the flames in my hands. Instead of burning my hands, they turned into what looked like small fireballs.

"Whaaat?"

I lightly tossed them in my hands and realized they were light as feathers. I put them together and made an even bigger one. I focused and was able to make them turn to smoke. With some more concentration, I was able to make some more. Soon, I didn't need to hold them anymore, and I'd found a way to make them hover on their own. I was just playing with them when I accidentally dropped one, and the carpet caught fire. I was able to put it out by just concentrating. I just looked at it, honestly. It wasn't long before my parents got home.

When they did, the first thing they did was make dinner. All they did was cast a spell, even though it's a lot more fun to cook it yourself, even if you use magic to prepare it. Of course, I'd given up explaining that to them a long time ago. They called me down to dinner, and I happily raced downstairs to greet them.

"Hey, Sammy." They said together.

"Hey, guys! What's for dinner tonight?"

"Spaghetti," they said.

"Sweet," I said, taking my seat at the dinner table.

During dinner, we went through the whole 'What-did-you-do-today' conversation. Obviously, I didn't tell them anything, but the more I thought about it, the more I realized how absolutely crazy my day had been. I had met Charlotte, Alex, Eliza, and Sabrina. Before that, I got screamed at for showing up late to class. *After* that, I found that there's something weird about pretty much all of my teachers. At home, I found that I can travel in my sleep, turn to smoke, and to top it all off, make fireballs.

That night, I lay awake in bed. Thinking. Wondering. Did the others have powers? Or was it just Charlotte and me? What else could Charlotte and I do? What had caused this to happen? Then a sickening thought struck me. Had this all just been a dream?

I sat up in bed and experimentally pinched myself. I heaved a sigh of relief when I felt the pain and laid back down. I turned on my side and looked out my window at the starry night sky; it was just beautiful. I pictured a witch's silhouette riding her broom past the full moon like a shooting star. With that thought, I slowly drifted off into a deep, dreamless sleep.

CHAPTER 11

Charlotte

Once Sam hung up, my siblings warily came downstairs. They gave me a weird look like I was crazy or something.

"Why are you looking at me like that?"

They looked at each other, then back at me.

"Who were you talking to?" My brother asked.

"Sam from school. He was just asking me something-"

"No. We mean in your room. You were talking, but there wasn't anyone there."

I was confused. "What are you talking about? He was right" What they said made me think. Sam had said that he suddenly woke up on his roof, and my siblings said that they hadn't seen him at all.

Maybe Sam hadn't really been here at all. The more I thought about it, the more I realized he didn't look *whole* when I'd seen him. It was almost like he was a spirit or ghost. Maybe his soul had left his body when he went to sleep. Then, his soul is what came to my house rather than Sam himself.

I started to call Sam back, but it was getting late, so I decided to call it a day.

"Sorry, guys. I..." I wasn't sure what to say. "Don't worry about it." Before they could ask any questions, I flew past them into my room. I finished all of my homework and decided to experiment with my newfound magic. I took off my hat, and with some concentration, I was able to make it fly on its own. I held it in my hands and closed my eyes. When I opened them, my hat was being lifted by some kind of wind. I moved my hands, and the hat followed. That's when I realized my *hands* were causing the wind.

My hat stopped hovering and landed in my hands. Experimentally, I set my hat on my bed, hopped off, and thrust my hands towards it. My hat flung itself against the wall instantly. I stared speechless at it until I finally brought it back to me. I put my hat on my head and smiled in my mirror. This was going to be fun.

That night, I had a strange dream. I was in the hallway at school. It was dark and deserted with only a few lights on. Two shone brightly on me, and a faint red one glowed from the end of the hall. I noticed it slowly got brighter, little by little.

"Oh, Charlotte," the woman called with a thundering yet calm voice, "It looks like your time is up." She cackled wickedly as the red light faded. I looked around, and everywhere I turned, an enormous boulder was hovering, ready to strike. I tried to run, but I couldn't move. I stood there in terror, as the rocks began to spiral around me.

"Chaar-lotte!" The woman's crackle echoed through the halls. The rocks kept spinning faster and faster, and the voice kept getting louder and louder until.

"Charlotte!"

I opened my eyes to find my nose a foot away from my ceiling. I reached for my sheets, but my hand just swatted through the air. I turned onto my stomach and found that I was floating close to five feet above my bed. I slammed into it so hard it nearly broke, and I was pretty sure the house shook.

I unburied myself from inside my pillows to find both of my awestruck siblings staring at me. I just sighed, got out of bed, and shut my door, so I could get dressed. When I opened my door again, they were already in the kitchen eating in silence. They stared at me as I came in. With a plate of french toast already at my seat, I sat down and began to eat. Nobody said a word.

At least for the next thirty seconds.

"Okay!" Amber said, slamming down her spatula, "What were you doing in your room? It sounded like there was a tornado or something!"

Brian nodded in agreement, "And when we came in there, you were floating! It's that spell you cast on your bed the other night, wasn't it?" I just shook my head and kept chewing.

To be honest, their questions were the least of my concern. I was still a bit shaken up about my dream, and I couldn't stop thinking about it. That woman, screaming my name. Those boulders were what really caught my attention. They all looked just like the one on my roof. This all could've been some bad dream, but I wasn't too sure. I was still thinking about what it could all mean when I realized my siblings were still talking.

Instead of trying to listen, I just cut them off.

"Guys, I don't know anything about what happened this morning. I *do* know that I have a long day at school to get to, so if you'll excuse me," I got out of my chair and looked up at the clock. "I'm going to start now." I held out my hands, and my belt and broom flew to me. Before my siblings could respond, I hopped onto my broom and flew out to the bus stop.

Why did I fly on my broom after I knew I could fly? I didn't fully trust my "abilities" yet. It's a lot easier to be confident in your flying when you have your bed as a landing pad.

Once I got to my seat at the back of the bus, I had an idea. I held out one hand and made swirling motions above it with my other one. After a moment, a small tornado began to form. I cupped it in both of my hands and watched in amazement as it kept spinning. I was still staring at my mini-tornado when Eliza plopped down beside me. Startled, I jumped in my seat, and my tornado immediately dissipated.

"Hey, Charlotte!" the twins said.

"Oh! Hey guys."

"So…is your roof fixed?" Alex asked.

"Well, no. Not exactly, but we did move the boulder… sorta." I explained how the boulder nearly crushed me but left out the fact that it was because my siblings didn't follow my advice.

By the end of it, Alex and Eliza looked pale.

"But guys, don't worry about it! I'm fine, see? Not a scratch. Besides, I kept it from hitting me. Turns out, I have-" I stopped myself. I hadn't intended to tell anyone about my "powers" or whatever. But since I had already started talking, there wasn't much point in stopping now.

"Some kind of magic powers," I finished.

The twins gasped, and I thought they were going to accuse me of lying. To my surprise, they instead said, "We do too!"

Alex held out his hand. At first, nothing happened, but then a small sapling grew from his palm. In an instant, there was a gorgeous, purple rose in his hand, which he then gave to me. I gratefully took it and held it up to my nose. It smelled sweet like honey, and I hoped it would last forever.

"Alex, this is beautiful!"

"My turn," Eliza said. She cupped her hands together, and a water bubble formed. It got as large as her palms before she dropped it on her head. A few drops splashed on me, but that wasn't my biggest concern. I sat there, staring at Eliza's completely dry hair.

"Woah."

I noticed the twins looking at me expectantly, and I got the message. I thought about the trick I had done earlier and made a miniature tornado in my palm. Both of them stared at my hands in amazement.

"I know, right? I just learned it this morning! Turns out, I can also fly, and I think I have telekinesis."

"Really? All I know is that I can make vines," Alex said.

"Yeah, and *poison ivy*." Eliza pulled up her sleeves, revealing a dark red rash with a few marks from previous scratches. Alex's hand went to the back of his neck.

"Yeah, that's my bad. I was trying to tickle her with vines, but I didn't mean for them to be poisoned."

Eliza stuck her tongue out at him, and I laughed.

"Maybe Sabrina's grandmother will have some ointment or something."

Eliza pulled her sleeve back down.

"Yeah. Maybe."

"So, Charlotte. Why didn't you answer when Sabrina called?"

I was confused. "Sabrina called? I don't remember hearing anything. Wait. I must've been on my roof..."

Alex looked kind of relieved, and I thought I heard Eliza mutter, "I told you so."

The next thing we knew, we were at school. We were mingling in the hallways when there was a sudden flash of light. Nobody else in the hall seemed to notice, which was strange since it filled most of the hallway. We had to cover our eyes to keep from being blinded.

Before I could uncover my eyes, I was nearly tackled to the ground with a hug.

"Charlotte! Thank you, thank you, thank you!" Sabrina said ecstatically.

I squeezed her back as the twins cautiously moved their arms that were still over their eyes.

"What was that?" Alex asked.

"Um...what was what?" Sabrina responded.

"I'm going to go out on a limb here and assume that you made that light, but what are you thanking Charlotte for?"

I froze as Sabrina quickly unwrapped her arms from around me.

"Well, Charlotte helped me find my neighbor's dog. That I was watching over." She smiled at me. "If it wasn't for her, I may have never found it."

I just nodded in agreement since I was terrible at lying. Thankfully, nobody had time to ask any more questions because Sam showed up in a cloud of smoke.

"Hey, guys. Sup?"

We all greeted him and together went to our lockers. Sabrina asked me about the survey, and I told her that I hadn't finished it yet. So we went to homeroom, and Sabrina filled out my survey for me. The second I took it out, she had begun filling in the answers. I tried to protest, but by then, she had already finished.

"How did you do that so fast?"

"Oh! Well, ...you wouldn't believe me if I told you."

I put my hand on her shoulder.

"Listen. You can tell us anything, but first, let me guess." I pretended to be deep in thought. "You've suddenly got some crazy powers that gave you super speed."

She stared at me in amazement.

"H-how'd you know?"

I held up my palm and made a tornado.

"Lucky guess."

We all proceeded to show Sabrina how we all found these crazy new abilities, including Sam. Only instead of turning into a smoke cloud-like, he had before, he made two fireballs in his hands.

"Cool, huh?"

Before anyone could respond, the bell rang, and we were off to first period. Throughout first period, I noticed Mr. Thornheart seemed to be keeping a close eye on Sam and me. He had just told us to take out our homework and our extra reading books when I realized I'd left mine at home.

I began to panic. Thornheart already thought I was in trouble, and he didn't have the best temper. I figured coming unprepared to class might make him have another one of those "episodes." Sam seemed to notice because he asked what was wrong. I told him I'd left my book at home, and he volunteered to go get it.

"What? No!" I whisper shouted. "It's not that big of a deal," I saw Thornheart glaring at me, "I hope."

"I can get it, though. I learned some kind of teleportation

trick or something this morning. I'll be in and out."

I hesitated. Why was he always being so risky? Thornheart already seemed to have it out for both of us, but eventually, I gave in.

"Fine. It's on my bed."

He leaned back and raised his hand until Mr. Thornheart reluctantly called on him.

"May I use the restroom?"

Thornheart sighed, "Now? Fine. Just hurry back."

Sam got up, and the second Thornheart turned his back, he winked at me and disappeared into the table's shadow.

Everyone at our table gasped, immediately grabbing the teacher's attention.

"What is it?"

We all stared at him, silent, until Eliza said, "We thought we saw a bird. That's all."

He glared at me and went to scolding at another student with chewing gum. We all heaved a breath of relief, and Sabrina asked me where Sam went.

"I left my book, so he went to go get it."

She just nodded, and we finally began to listen to Thornheart. Well...sort of. I don't remember a thing he said, but I do remember eyeing the clock. Five minutes passed, and there was no sign of Sam. Seven minutes. Ten. I was starting to get worried.

Had he gotten lost? Had he accidentally went through a wormhole? Or what if he was just tricking me, and he wasn't really getting my book? What if he was going through all of my things?

A horrible thought struck me. What if he was after my spellbook?

I tried to shake the thought, but it was stuck in my brain.

I was busy trying to remind myself that I already had it with me, I was starting to second guess myself when I felt a tap on my shoulder. I looked towards Sabrina, who simply gestured towards the table. Confused, I looked at the table, and then nearly fell out of my seat. A tornado, over half my size, was whirling on top of the table. As I panicked, it spun faster and faster. Kids began to turn our way, and I knew it wouldn't be long before Thornheart noticed too.

In a panic, I reached out and waved my hand through the twister. It immediately dissipated, just before Thornheart turned to see what was going on.

"What is all this ruckus about?"

I was still reaching across the table, frozen in fear. I quickly sat back down and thought of the first thing that came to mind.

"I, um...dropped my book?"

He glared at me, and I realized the whole class was staring me down too. I felt their eyes watching me, and it made me want to disappear. It felt like the silence lasted forever, but then Thornheart finally turned away. The second he did, Sam stepped out of a shadow on the floor. Luckily, everyone seemed to have lost interest in our table by then. Before he could say a word, I put my fingers to my lips, signaling for him to stay quiet.

He gave me my book, and I tried to act like I was reading. My hands were shaking, and I could hardly read the words on the pages. There was something about the attention that seemed to terrify me. My head filled with thoughts of what the kids must've been thinking about me. How crazy I looked. What my problem was. Why I was such a troublemaker.

Then I felt another tap on my shoulder. I sighed and in my head, told the tornado to dissipate without looking up. After what seemed like forever, the bell rang, and we began to pack up our things. Boy, I was not looking forward to explaining the tornados. I was, however, looking forward to Sam's explanation as to why it took him almost twenty minutes to find a book on my bed.

CHAPTER 12

Alexander

Apparently, Charlotte makes tornados when she gets nervous. At least, that's what she told us. I asked her on our way to our lockers.

"So, Charlotte...What happened in there?"

She hesitated, and I immediately regretted asking.

"Well...Sam just had me a little worried. After all," She turned to him as we walked, "it did take you almost *twenty minutes* to get a book."

Sam pretended to look offended.

"Well, I'm *sorry* that you have one of the cutest cats ever."

"Wait. You spent twenty minutes playing with Charlotte's cat?" Sabrina asked.

Sam just shrugged, while Charlotte turned back around.

"So, what *did* happen in class while I was gone?"

"Charlotte made two tornadoes," Eliza said casually.

"What?! Cool! I can't believe I missed that!"

Charlotte seemed to look a bit uncomfortable, and I noticed the other students watching us as we walked. Charlotte tensed as students began to whisper. To avoid another tornado, I walked faster to stay with her, and I tried to strike up a conversation.

"So, you...have a cat?"

She seemed startled by my voice at first, but then she smiled.

"Yeah. Her name is Dawn. She's really sweet and always seems to know when I need to be cheered up."

We had lost ourselves in a conversation about different pets when we found ourselves in class. We sat down at our table and waited for the others to join us. When they finally did, we decided to talk about our powers, since Charlotte was relaxed again. While we were talking, I noticed something shining on her wrist.

"Hey, Charlotte." I pointed to her wrist, "What's that?"

She pulled back her sleeve and revealed a black stringed bracelet with what looked like a broken pearl white bead on it.

"This is a bracelet that my mom gave me when I turned ten. I promised not to take it off, and I never have."

I asked her if it had always been broken, and she nodded. Then Sam got a closer look at it, and he gasped.

"No way! I have the same bead!"

He pulled back his sleeve and showed a similar bracelet on his wrist. It also had a broken pearly bead, but it also had a sliver of a black pearl on it.

Charlotte gasped as well, and they put their beads together. They were a perfect fit, but there still seemed to be a large chunk of it missing.

They both seemed too excited to notice, though.

After calling attendance, the teacher asked for our surveys. She told us that we would be put in groups with students whose answers were close to our own. We all glanced at Sabrina with glad-we-listened-to-you looks. She smiled happily, and the teacher continued.

She said that our groups will be displayed on the board, and once they were, we were to find our group members and sit at a table together.

"*Disponere!*" she said, aiming her wand at the neatly stacked surveys. The papers began to throw themselves into her whiteboard. Each time a survey hit the board, a person's name took its place. They started forming columns, and sure enough, all of our names were in a column.

"Alright then! These are your groups," she gestured towards the board with her hands, "so get with 'em!"

Kids happily joined their friends in their new groups while we all stayed put. Once they all got situated, we officially began our class assignment. The assignment was to solve five puzzles, and whoever finished them all first, with the most accuracy, would win. I don't know about you, but prize or not, I play to win!

Charlotte seemed to have the right idea because she was already making plans.

"How about we split up the puzzles, but still work together? Alex and I can work on two, while you guys work together on the other three. If you finish before us, or vise versa, then we'll come together and work on whatever's left. Sound like a plan?"

Everyone nodded in agreement.

"It's settled then."

We turned our attention back to our teacher, who had five stacks of paper hovering in front of her.

"Well, if everyone is ready," she hesitated for suspense, "let's begin!"

A sheet of paper from each stack flew onto each table, and Charlotte quickly grabbed two and got started. Let me just say, Charlotte, and I make a fantastic team. Still, I have to give Charlotte most of the credit. With her on our side, the others didn't stand a chance. It was fun working with her. She was so excited to solve the puzzles, too, and she would even stop to make sure I got a crack at it. She was just so selfless.

Anyway, we obviously were the first to finish, but we had to wait until the end of class to determine who won on accuracy. I was positive we'd won, but Charlotte didn't look so sure.

"Do you think we won?" she asked me a few minutes after we'd turned our puzzles in.

"Yeah. After all, we've got you on our team."

She smiled, but still looked anxious.

I wasn't sure what else I could do to comfort her, so we waited for the results in silence. It was about another five-minute wait, but the other groups finished and turned in their puzzles. Nobody seemed to notice that we had finished first because the teams after us were celebrating once they turned theirs in. Maybe they were just as confident as I was. There was no way to be sure until the results came in.

Right before she told us who won, she asked each group to make up a team name. Someone asked why she hadn't let us make names in the beginning, but she didn't answer. Instead, she warned us that we had about two minutes.

"Any ideas?" I asked the group.

Everyone shrugged except for Charlotte.

"Maybe we can...make an acronym? With our names."

"Let's see...C, E, S, A, S... I've got it! A.C.E.S.!" Sam exclaimed.

"You're missing another S," Eliza pointed out.

"How about C.A.S.E.S.?" Charlotte suggested.

"Oh! *Magic* C.A.S.E.S.!" Sabrina added.

"Perfect," Charlotte and I said in unison.

She laughed as I blushed furiously and yanked off my hat.

When the time came, we announced our group name with pride.

"Okay, then. The results are in, and the winning group is..."

"*Magic C.A.S.E.S.!*"

We whooped and hollered, at a reasonable volume, excited that we'd won our first contest as a group. She announced the second and third place winners too, but we didn't care all that much. We were just happy that we'd won.

The whole way to third period, we spoke about nothing but *Magic C.A.S.E.S.*'s first victory. Everyone in the art room was buzzing, curious what today's assignment would be. The art teacher appeared suddenly from behind the door, scaring the last student to come in.

"Good morning, children! Today we will be carving animal statues..."

The class seemed rather excited until she finished her sentence.

"From *scratch*!"

"What?!?" the whole class echoed.

Everyone was surprised. Even I was, and that never happens at school!

"That's right! In fact, I'll be collecting your wands tomorrow when we get started. For now, you will simply be sketching out your ideas."

We were no longer excited about the assignment. After all, we were sorcerers. Magic wasn't something we usually went without. Still, we sketched out our ideas as instructed. I decided I was going to carve an owl. They were beautiful, smart, brave birds. When they fly, their wings fill the night sky, and their feathers practically reflect the moonlight.

The funny thing is, I found myself referring to Charlotte as I sketched. I used her dark brown hair to help me draw the feathers. Her eyes for the owl. I even added glasses to it. The owl would be nobly perched onto a rock as though it had just performed a heroic act. Once I finished, I asked Charlotte what she thought about it and what animal she was carving.

"Woah. That's so realistic, and I love the glasses! They look just like mine! I'm carving my cat, Dawn. Eliza said she was going to carve a dolphin, and I think Sam said he was carving a Golden retriever." She turned and called down the table, "Hey, Sabrina...what animal are you doing?" I didn't hear what she said, but it didn't matter because Charlotte told me anyway.

"She said she was doing a rabbit."

"Cool."

"So, why an owl?"

"Hm?"

"Why are you doing an owl? Like, do you see them ever? I've never seen one in person, but I've read about them. I've even seen pictures. They're so pretty!"

"Maybe I could take you to see one sometime!" I blurted out and instantly was filled with regret.

"Really? You...think you could?"

"Y-yeah! I live right over a forest. I'm sure I could find one for you to see."

"That'd be awesome!"

"Yeah, it would be."

Now that I'd gotten her all excited, Charlotte spent the rest of class doodling pictures of owls. I caught a glimpse of some of them. That was when I realized that Charlotte is a much better artist than me.

CHAPTER 13

Sabrina

I was looking forward to lunch because I'd be able to cast the spell that Sam taught us the day before. I took my wand and carefully said the spell, expecting it to go horribly wrong. To my surprise, it worked perfectly. I tried not to over-react, but I'm pretty sure I didn't do that well.

"So, did you guys get permission to come over today?"

Everyone nodded.

"Sweet! So, just so you know, I live with my grandmother. We don't have any pets or anything, so if you have allergies, it's not a problem. She also likes to cook things in her cauldron like soup and tea and whatnot. Obviously, she still uses it for po-tions, which is why I'm usually hesitant to drink her tea, but I'm not implying anything! Her tea's delicious actually, and her po-tions never go wrong as far as I know. Still, it's not like she'd tell me if anything went wrong, but you can trust her."

They all just stared at me until Charlotte put a gentle hand on my shoulder.

"Sabrina. I think I speak for all of us when I say that I didn't understand about ninety percent of what you just said."

They all nodded.

"So repeat what you just said, but slower."

"Okay," so I said it all again, but slower.

"Good to know."

We all sat in silence for a while, not sure what to talk about. At least until Sam decided to tell a joke.

"What do you call a sad coffee?"

Nobody knew.

"A depresso!"

Eliza snickered while the rest of us just stared at him.

"Oh! I get it!" Charlotte said after a while. Then she began chuckling for a minute before the silence resumed.

"So..."

I decided to try and break the awkward silence.

"My...grandma might...be able to explain our powers."

"Really?" Charlotte asked.

"Yeah. I asked her when I got mine if she had any ideas. At first, she thought it was the tea she gave me, but then there was the possibility it might've been elemental magic."

"Elemental magic?" Everyone asked at once.

"Look, my grandma could explain it better than me, so I'll ask her about it after school."

After lunch, we went to class, and we all took out our flowers from the night before. Everyone except Alex. I took out my potted sunflower and asked him where his was.

"Um," He held out his hand, "right here!"

Suddenly a sunflower appeared in his hand.

I stared at it, confused, before simply giving up on trying to comprehend it.

I was extremely excited about this class because I'd get to cast spells, something I still wasn't used to.

I got to work with Richard this time, and I was super excited that I could participate. To be honest, I hardly remember the assignment. I do, however, remember how much fun I had with Richard. Luckily, I was able to hold a normal conversation that didn't start with me running into him. I was quite disappointed that it had to end.

Turns out, he might have cool powers too. Well, he didn't tell me exactly, but I did notice that he didn't have a shadow. I wanted to ask him about it, but I decided not to. I figured my eyes were playing tricks on me or something.

At the end of class, he handed me a rose and said, "Stay cool, Sabrina," right before the bell rang. I sat there dumbfounded as everyone filed out of the room. Charlotte had to tap me on the shoulder.

"Sabrina. The bell rang."

"Oh! Right!" I said dumbly as I packed up my things. I was being extra careful not to damage the rose when I realized that I never saw Richard leave the room. He told me to stay cool, I blinked, and he was gone.

I walked out and caught up with the others. Sam and Eliza were in a conversation between themselves already. Same with Alex and Charlotte, so I just walked to class in silence.

During transportation, the teacher kept a pretty close eye on Alex and Charlotte while he explained the assignment. We went outside that day to work on antigravity spells. We had to leave our spell books inside and make up the spells ourselves. We all worked together in one big group. We had no idea how we were going to do this. Well, as usual, all but one. This time it was Charlotte.

"Guys, you know, we don't have to do anything, right?"

"Huh?" we asked at once

"I have telekinesis."

"*Ohhh*," We all said.

She just laughed and asked for something to 'cast a spell on.'

I picked up a rock and handed it to her.

"Perfect."

She took the stone just as our teacher came to check on our progress.

"Goofing off now, are we?"

"Not at all, sir. In fact, we just cast a spell on this rock, but I think it needs an activator. A powerful wizard such as yourself might just do the trick."

She placed the stone in his hand before he could respond.

He immediately dropped it to the ground. At first, it stayed there, but then it slowly began to hover, then float, then fly.

It flew over the roof and disappeared while our teacher stared at the sky in disbelief.

"I guess we're done then."

"W-well, not yet! Just...keep practicing, or something!"

"Yes, sir," we said politely.

We watched him walk away, dumbfounded.

"So...now what?" I asked.

"Now, *we* fly!"

Before I could respond, I was lifted off the ground. I wasn't scared, just surprised. I couldn't really control where I went, but I found myself just enjoying it. We kept going up, higher and higher. Well, not *too* high. About five and a half feet. I guess that was when we got a bit rowdy. Rowdy enough to get the teacher over to us.

"What is going on?!"

We all stopped laughing.

"Um...we think someone cast their spell on us by mistake," Eliza told him.

"Yeah," we all agreed.

"W-well... I'd better go find a reversal spell. Don't go anywhere!"

With a blink of the eye, the teacher disappeared. As soon as he was gone, Charlotte set us down. Then, the teacher appeared in front of us again, carrying his spellbook.

"What in the-"

"The spell wore off," I told him.

Having given up, he sighed and went back to work with the other kids. Once he was out of earshot, we all burst into a fit of laughter.

"That was awesome!" I declared.

"Yeah!"

"We should do that again sometime."

"Maybe, just not anytime soon," Charlotte said.

That's when I looked over and saw how tired Charlotte

looked. She was laying against the side of the building, sweating, and seemingly catching her breath.

"Charlotte, are you okay?"

Everyone turned to her, but she just nodded.

"Yeah, I'm fine. Just kinda tired. Who knew you guys would be so heavy?"

Before I could say another word, Charlotte was fast asleep. We let her rest while keeping a lookout for the teacher until the end of class. When the teacher announced that it was time to head inside, I gently shook her awake. She woke up, and we all went inside together before anyone noticed she'd been napping.

Once we were all packed up, we all went outside just like all of the other kids, but we just stood there.

"So, Sabrina…now what?" Sam asked me after a few moments.

"Hold on. I'm trying to wait for more kids to leave. I have a spell that I'd hate to cast on the wrong person."

"Spell? What spell?" The twins asked in unison.

"Don't worry. My grandma gave it to me. It'll send you guys straight to our house." Having eased their nerves, we waited in silence for the kids to leave. Soon it was just us, and a few others left.

"Okay," I said, taking out the slip of paper with the spell on it. "Get ready."

They all straightened up, ready for travel, and I told them to stand in a straight line. When they did, I read the spell aloud.

"*Tolle eas in domum meam.*"

With a sudden flash of light, all four of them were gone.

I flipped the slip over and read the spell to get me home aloud.

"*Suscipe me in,*" and in a flash of light, I was at home, surrounded by all of my friends.

"Hey!" they all said when I appeared.

I smiled and led them to my front door.

"So, welcome to my home!"

I gave them a quick tour of my house. I showed them my room, the basement, the bathroom, and the kitchen before taking them outside to see my treehouse.

"There it is! Go ahead, climb in."

They stared in amazement as though they'd never seen a treehouse before. That's when it occurred to me that may have been the case.

"Um, follow me," I told them as I raced up the ladder.

They followed me up the ladder so quickly that they almost ran over each other. Charlotte flew through one of the windows to give the others more room.

"Woah," they all said in unison.

"Yup. This is it… I'm gonna go get some snacks. Stay here," I said before I ran back out to the kitchen. My grandma, who's always one step ahead of me, already had a plate of snacks on the table.

"Thanks, Grandma!"

"Of course, dear, but I think I'd like to meet your friends."

"Right! But that reminds me…I think they have elemental magic, just like me."

She froze and stared at me.

"It can't be…" She murmured. "Sabrina, please bring me to your friends."

She grabbed the plate of snacks, and I led her outside. I called my friends to come down and meet her. They climbed down the ladder, single file, and I introduced each of them.

"So, my grandma would like to see your powers." She nodded, and Sam took a step forward. He held out his fists, and they quickly burst into flames. We watched in amazement as he immediately put them back out.

"I can also do this," he said before disappearing and leaving behind a cloud of smoke. Then he reappeared while the smoke cloud vanished.

My grandmother just nodded, but she seemed kind of concerned.

Then, Alex stepped forward and turned toward the treehouse. Then he thrust his hands towards it, and long leafy vines appeared and wrapped themselves around the trunk.

He turned back towards grandma and raised his hand upward. As he did, a giant leaf erupted from the ground. "I...can do that too."

Eliza held out her hand with a water bubble in it.

"I can pretty much only do this," she said before splashing her head with it and staying completely dry.

Charlotte was hovering already, and with a slight upward motion, she made all four of us fly with her. After a few seconds, she set us back down and said, "That's what I can do."

Grandma just stood there and stared at us.

"Oh no, oh no, oh no..." She muttered. "Come with me, children. There is something I must tell you," she said as she led us back inside.

We all stood around while Grandma ran off in search of a book. Knowing which book she was looking for, I ran and got it for her. She opened it and read the pages aloud.

"Every thousand years, a group of young sorcerers will come together and use their powers to protect nature's hidden elements from falling into the wrong hands. These-"

"Wait. Are *we* these kids?" Eliza asked.

"Unfortunately, it seems so," my grandma said.

"What does it mean 'nature's hidden elements'?" Sam asked.

"Well, ...you possess some of nature's most powerful magical elements already. Fire, wind, water, flora, and lightning. There are many other elements out there, such as ice, magma, metal, and even wildlife, the element of animals."

"So, we have to protect these elements from...what exactly?" Charlotte asked.

"Well, your powers are 'activated,' so to speak, once your enemy finds you, so if you have these powers now, an evil force has already discovered you."

Everyone looked uneasy.

"You will have to fight this force and protect your elements from falling into the wrong hands. You may even fight this force with elements of their own. In fact," she shut her book. "Your training should start immediately!"

CHAPTER 14

Elizabeth

Honestly, I was pretty overwhelmed by all of this, I had about a hundred questions to ask, but I tried to limit them to two or less.

"So, what force are we going to fight?" I asked.

Sabrina's grandmother seemed unsure of how to respond.

"We should ask your ball!" Sabrina suggested.

"Sabrina, I doubt even my *crystal ball* could know such a thing." Her grandmother tried to protest, but she had already raced to the basement. Her grandmother sighed and started after her. We all followed her down the steps to find a faint grey light coming from the main room. As we walked down, we found Sabrina staring at a tall glowing mirror. I was about to ask her what she was looking at, but then I saw it for myself. There was a sorceress in the mirror peering into her cauldron. In the potion's reflection, we saw ourselves looking into a mirror. I rubbed my eyes, unsure of what I was seeing.

Then I got a better look at the sorceress, the supposed evil force looked quite young and kind of familiar.

"Wait. Is that our *dean*?!"

There was no denying it. Our dean, the person who'd been on my case since literal day one, was evil. *That explains all of the revenge nonsense*, I thought. But *what did she mean when she was talking about our ancestors?*

"Wait. Katara, is your grade's dean?" Her grandma asked.

"Who's Katara?" We all asked.

"Katara Apopano. An ancient sorceress who lived with the dinosaurs, back when all magicians had a much broader kind of elemental magic. She was disowned by her father, who back then was known as a 'Land Magician' because of her mixed magic. Her mother, being a 'Sky Magician,' raised her in the clouds, as a hatred for Land Magicians grew inside of Katara. Once she turned eighteen, she flew to the sky, and using her mixed magic sent a fleet of asteroids barreling towards Earth."

"So, that's what killed the dinosaurs?" Alex asked.

Her grandma nodded.

"These showers went on for days, all around the world. On the last day, she collapsed to the ground. The magicians of the world were furious. They'd been in hiding, trying to shelter as many animals as possible. They were led by two twin magicians with mixed magic of their own. Their names were Pan and Coventina.

My brother and I gasped.

"But those are *our* names!"

Everyone looked at us with confused looks.

"Well, technically, they're our middle names, but still!" I said

"That must be why she called us by our middle names the other day."

"And why she was saying all of that nonsense about our ancestors. She *knew* them personally."

"You can say that again. Your ancestors were the ones who saved her life."

"What?!" we all exclaimed in confusion.

"It's true. All of the magicians wanted Katara dead for what she did. All except for your ancestors. Just after Katara collapsed, the magicians surrounded her. Before they could do her any harm, the twins stepped in and came up with a more civilized solution. Community service."

"Really?" Charlotte asked.

"Absolutely. She was to help bury all of the dinosaur remains and fill up the craters from the shower after she destroyed all remaining rocks."

"But, that beats death, doesn't it? Why would she be mad at the twins?" Sabrina asked, but her grandmother simply shrugged.

"I have no idea. What I do know is she was supposed to have had her body sealed in the clouds. The problem is, your dean couldn't possibly be one of Katara's offspring because of how young she was when she passed."

"So what you're saying is that our dean is a million-year-old zombie who killed the dinosaurs," Sam said sarcastically.

"Pretty much."

We stood there in silence, trying to process all of this.

"Well!" Sabrina's grandmother clapped her hands together, "You'd better start training immediately. Who knows when Katara will strike."

"Let's just ask your ball," Sabrina suggested again.

Before her grandma could protest, Sabrina had asked the crystal ball when we were going to fight our dean. Instead of telling us, the ball showed us on a calendar that was projected onto the mirror.

"This *Friday*?!"

"Oh my! It couldn't possibly mean this Friday, can it?" Sabrina's grandmother said in disbelief, but there was no denying it. This Friday was highlighted on the calendar and had 'Big Brawl' written in red ink. Sabrina's grandma sighed in defeat.

"Wait! That's when the meteor shower is!" Sabrina exclaimed in horror.

"My goodness, you're right! That must be why she's fighting you on Friday! The asteroids... she's not only here to get revenge against the twins...she wants to destroy the Earth!"

We all stood there in disbelief.

Sabrina's grandmother turned to us gravely.

"I guess there's no denying it. Children, I hate to ask this of you, but I will need to see you all here every day after school for the rest of the week. And possibly the rest of the year."

We all nodded.

"Alright, then. I will see you all tomorrow. Good night children."

With that, she walked upstairs, and we all hesitated before following her. We all met in the kitchen and stood in silence until Charlotte said something.

"So, I guess we should go home now." We all agreed and said our goodbyes. Once we'd grabbed our brooms, we flew back home without a clue of what the future held for us.

When we got home, Alex and I went straight to our rooms. I plopped onto my bed without noticing Jordan.

"So, how was your day?" she asked. I ignored her, not in the mood to talk. She didn't say anything either, but I heard a weird tapping noise. I looked up and found Jordan with a laptop, typing away.

"Where did you get that?"

She didn't look up.

"It's a loaner."

"From school?"

"Yup."

"So.what'cha typing?"

"An essay."

I decided not to ask any more questions. I wanted to let her focus. Plus, I had to think of a way for me to ask my parents about Alex and I going back to Sabrina's house without mentioning the future of the planet depends on it.

At dinner, we all sat in silence.

"So, how was the girl's house?" our dad asked.

"It was fine," Alex said.

"Um...mom and dad, I was wondering," I looked at Alex. "Well, *we* were wondering if we could join this club at school. It's for a selective few who had good grades last year, and Alex and I were selected. They meet every day after school, so...we just need your permission."

"Oh. Well, of course, you can! This club sounds like such an honor! Who would we be to keep you from it?" my mother laughed.

Alex and I agreed and chuckled nervously.

"So, how long will this club go on?"

We stopped laughing.

"Um...they haven't told us yet. They said it might...go all year?"

My parents paused and exchanged weary glances.

I thought we were busted, but then they both nodded.

"That is alright. As long as you're both back by dinner."

We couldn't believe our luck! I didn't think they'd believe such a thing. That was the day that I learned that as long as I involved positive input about my grades, my parents were perfectly okay with it. But my excitement didn't last too long because I remembered why I lied in the first place. I had a battle to prepare for and a world to defend.

I didn't sleep well that night because I was so anxious. The next morning, Alex and I got ready without a single word to each other. We even waited at the bus stop in silence. It wasn't until Charlotte got on the bus that Alex heard my voice.

"So...Charlotte...how did you sleep last night?"

"Not that well...you?"

"Not well, either."

"Same here," Alex said.

"But, things should be fine, right? I mean, if we practice every day after school," Charlotte said.

"Right," Alex and I said, but we were still uneasy. We spent the rest of the bus ride in silence while we fooled around with our powers. I made water bubbles, Alex grew vines on the back of the seat, and Charlotte made miniature tornadoes.

Once we got to school, we met up with Sam and Sabrina outside of our lockers.

We were just about to say 'hi' when our dean walked by. We all froze as she gave Alex and me a death stare. When she walked away, Alex and I were still paralyzed with fear. After all, this woman *did* want us dead.

CHAPTER 15

Samuel

W hen Charlotte and the twins were coming over, I saw a familiar-looking teacher walk by. They all immediately froze until she went into a room and shut the door behind her. Then Charlotte quickly ran over to us, while the twins stared in silence at the door. When Charlotte came over, Sabrina asked what was up with the twins.

"Well…that was the dean, and she is pretty against them, so…"

"*Against* us? Ha! The understatement of the year!" Eliza said, having caught up to us.

"Yeah. She literally wants us *dead*," Alex reminded us.

At this point, I was confused.

"Wait. That teacher is the dean we're supposed to fight on Friday?"

Everyone stared at me like I was crazy before Charlotte put her hand on my shoulder.

"Yes. Yes, she is."

"Oh! Okay. Got it."

That's when I realized what made the teacher so familiar.

"Wait, Charlotte. Remember the dream I told you about the other day?"

"Um…yeah. What about it?"

"Well…the dean was in it. In fact, she was the one who put the boulder in your roof."

"What?! Why didn't you tell us sooner?!"

"I…at first I didn't recognize her. Then, I just wasn't sure, but…I am now."

Eliza just smiled at me as Charlotte stepped back.

"Well, thanks for telling us."

"Too bad we can't prove it or anything," Alex said.

"Actually, my grandma might know something about it. We'll have to ask her after school," Sabrina said before we all headed to homeroom.

Later, at lunch, everyone had brought their homework so that we could practice our powers after school. We worked in silence, trying to stay focused, but once we finished, nobody said anything. Since I wasn't very hungry, I hadn't gotten lunch. Neither had anyone else. I figured we were all just anxious for Friday.

I had gotten bored, so I decided to fool around with my magic. Obviously, when your element is fire, that usually isn't the best idea. I wasn't thinking, and I made a small fireball on the table. Keep in mind, this table is made entirely out of wood. I was kinda zoning out when I heard someone say my name. I looked up, and a corner of the table was engulfed in flames.

"Shoot!"

I tried to put them out with my hands, but that just made it worse. Everyone started panicking, and Eliza had to step in and put it out. She quickly put out the fire with a jet stream of water from her hands. It doused the fire, thankfully, and also soaked the table. Charlotte quickly dried it before anyone noticed what had happened. Once all was said and done, e just stared at each other, still in shock. Then, Sabrina began to laugh. Soon, we all joined in. I had lit a table on fire, Eliza had put it out, and Charlotte had cleared the evidence. Well…Alex had to grow the charred part back, so clearing the evidence was a team effort. We make a great team, don't we?

That afternoon at Sabrina's house, we were ready for battle. We stood in the backyard, single file, and awaited further instructions. Then, I heard someone shout something.

"Terra, surge!"

The ground shook beneath us, and five, enormous boulders suddenly broke from the ground. They lined up with each of us, and nobody moved. Then, Sabrina's grandmother marched out to the center of the yard.

"Katara is a sorceress with power over the earth. She can summon rocks from anywhere and manipulate them as she wishes. You need to be able to destroy these rocks before they can hurt you. That is what you will practice today."

With a flick of the wrist, the boulders were sent in our direction. At first, I panicked, but then I had an idea. I concentrated and blasted a jet of fire towards the boulder. It crumbled to the ground in a pile of ash.

"Piece of cake," I muttered before I suddenly began to feel light-headed. My vision blurred, and everything went dark. I woke up and looked around. Everyone was unconscious on the ground. I sat up and saw Sabrina's grandma cleaning up the broken pieces of rock left in the backyard. Soon the others started to wake up, and that's when I noticed that everyone's rocks had been smashed. I figured that was a good sign.

Once everyone woke up, Sabrina's grandmother had gone inside. We all went in after her, and she had a talk with us.

"I have no doubt that you are all capable of destroying Katara's rocks. I'm rather impressed with how easily you all did so. Luckily, you will be fighting together, so you shouldn't run out of energy like you did today. Still, you'll have to work on that tomorrow. But now it's getting dark, so you'd all better get home."

With that, we left, and at my house, I had a weird dream. I saw a cauldron full of bubbling, glowing, lime green liquid. I saw five children in the reflection, all soundly sleeping. All except two. A white boy my age was tossing and turning, and a young black girl was clutching her sheets. Suddenly, I heard a wicked cackling echo throughout the room. I looked up and saw Katara herself glaring at me. That's when I woke up in a cold sweat. It took me a while, but once my nerves had eased, I went back to sleep without any more interruptions.

CHAPTER 16

Charlotte

One last day before the big battle. I was terrified. To calm my nerves, I decided to hypnotize myself with mini tornados. I was so mesmerized, I didn't even notice the twins come on the bus. It wasn't until they directly asked me if I was okay that I saw them.

"Huh? What? Oh. Hey guys!"

They gave me a concerned look.

"Are you...worried about tomorrow?" They asked in unison.

"W-well...I mean, kinda?" I sighed, "Heck yeah. I'm terrified. After all, it's not every day that you find yourself fighting someone who wants to destroy you *and* your planet."

They nodded.

"We are too," they said in unison.

"B-but, we should be fine! As long as we work together, right?"

They nodded warily, and we sat in silence for the rest of the bus ride. In first period, I couldn't concentrate. My mind wandered every few seconds, so it wasn't long before I got an infraction. Apparently, the teacher had called me twice for attendance. Clearly, he thought I was ignoring him, so I now had Friday detention. To be honest, I didn't care too much. After all, I was going to end up with the dean on Friday, one way or another.

Still, Alex tried to comfort me.

"Hey, Charlotte! Don't worry about your infraction. We're all seeing the dean tomorrow, so it's fine."

Before I could tell him that I was fine, I heard a teacher call out to him.

"Pan! That's an infraction, mister!" the dean was pointing at something behind us. We turned and saw Alex's broom hovering directly behind me.

"What? How did that get there?" Alex asked, completely dumbfounded.

"Nice try. That act isn't fooling anyone. Friday detention!" the dean declared. She shoved a pink slip of paper into his chest and walked away, cackling.

I looked at him, and he looked at me. We were both perplexed. I looked behind him and saw that his broom was gone.

"What in the clouds?"

Then, I looked back in the dean's direction and saw "his" broom dutifully hovering behind her. I balled up my fists and started after her...
but Alex quickly grabbed my wrist.

I turned, glaring at him, and he immediately let go.

"Sorry! It's just...the infraction isn't that big a deal. I mean...we're gonna fight her tomorrow, so...we can get her back then."

I opened my fists and sighed.

"You're right. I'm sorry, I was...out of line."

He smiled.

"It's okay," he said, and we quickly went to our next class. I was looking forward to today's puzzles. They were an excellent way to relax and clear my mind. Sabrina was excited too. So excited that she accidentally used her super speed on one of them. When we turned them in, one of the other groups accused us of cheating. They said we'd cast a spell on Sabrina so she'd finish earlier.

"Is this true?" the teacher asked.

Before any of us could protest, Sabrina stood up and defended herself. While talking with super speed, nobody could understand a word that she said. She sat down and crossed her arms when she was done. The teacher just looked at her before sighing.

"I'm sorry, but *Magic C.A.S.E.S.* is disqualified. Sabrina that's an infraction for you."

Sabrina wanted to protest, but I put my hand on her shoulder to keep her from getting up. She sat back down, but I could tell she was still mad. Still, I apologized to her at the end of class before we left.

"Why in the world would you apologize? It's not like I can help it!" Sabrina asked as we left class.

"Well, as unfair as it is, there's no point in arguing about it," I reminded her. "After all, we'll be seeing the dean tomorrow anyways."

She sighed.

"Yeah, you're right."

"Besides," Sam began to add, "how are we supposed to explain that you naturally have super speed to the teacher?"

"Okay! Okay! I get it!"

We laughed as we continued down the hall, but I couldn't help but wonder whether or not these infractions were coincidental.

CHAPTER 17

Alexander

As we walked to class, I noticed that Charlotte seemed kind of unsettled.

"Hey, what's on your mind?"

"Oh, nothing," she said, sounding skeptical.

"I'm just wondering...are all these infractions a coincidence? What if they're intended to *ensure* that we get stuck with the dean tomorrow?"

I didn't know what to say. If that was the case, then what? Detention would be unavoidable, but we knew what had to be done anyway.

"What if we are all on our absolute **best** behavior for the next few periods?" My sister suggested. "That way, if we don't do anything wrong and we *still* get infractions, we know that it's out of our control!"

"Good idea!" Sam said. "After all, we're the only ones left to get them, so this shouldn't be too hard."

Of course, that was said soon before Sam sneezed a fireball onto a student's table during class. He got an infraction for it too.

"Okay, I'm not sure what that counts as," Eliza said after class.

"Neither do I. I mean, how am I supposed to control a

sneeze?"

We all shrugged.

"Welp, I guess it's up to you, Eliza," Sabrina said as we went off to lunch.

They served spaghetti; we had lasagna and discussed battle strategies.

"Okay, so we know the dean works with rocks. So we have to be able to destroy those rocks and fight *her* without completely draining ourselves."

"Right. We also need to be able to defend ourselves."

"Who here has the best form of protection?"

I slowly raised my hand.

"My leaves can grow pretty big. They're strong enough to be used as shields. Maybe I could give each of you one before we fight.

"Good idea!"

"Okay, now fighting back?"

Sabrina and Sam raised their hands.

"I can blast 'em," they said in unison.

Everyone turned to Eliza and Charlotte.

"Well, I'm not sure how much of a help I could be. I mean...I can always make a tornado around her. That would *definitely* distract her," Charlotte suggested.

"I could splash her with water...hopefully, it will be more effective than it sounds," Eliza said.

"Well, if that fails, I'm sure there's something else you could do," Sam said reassuringly.

She smiled, and we went back to eating lunch.

When we went to the next period, I could tell Eliza was trying her best not to provoke anyone in the room. In fact, when she felt like she was about to sneeze, she quickly went to the restroom. When she came back, another girl hurriedly rushed out behind her. Once the girl got to the door, she was splashed on the head with water. The whole class gasped as my sisters, and I exchanged looks of disbelief.

"What the hex was that for?" the girl demanded.

"B-but I didn't do that!" My sister held up her hands defensively.

"Oh yeah? Then what were you mumbling? And why are your hands wet?"

Eliza looked at her hands. To her dismay, she saw that they were dripping wet.

But...how? I wondered. *Her hand's don't get wet...do they?*

Eliza looked to us for support, but we were as shocked as she was.

"I-I just got back from the restroom. Of course, they're wet!"

"She's just using that as a cover-up! There are dryers in there!"

The teacher stood up.

"Eliza! Apologize immediately!"

"B-but I didn't-"

"You will already be seeing the dean tomorrow in detention, do *not* make me send you to the principal!"

Eliza hesitated before apologizing to the girl.

The girl walked out the door, and I saw Eliza swiftly flick her wrist before shutting the door behind her.

She sat down next to me, and for a moment, her hat seemed to smoke. Then, it returned to its usual color, and she smiled smugly.

The girl never came back from the restroom, but the teacher didn't seem to notice. I, however, realized that I'd never seen the girl before. Not in class or in the hall the days before. I decided I'd bring it to the group's attention later. Eliza got her infraction from the teacher. When she came outside, I asked her what she'd been smiling about earlier.

She just turned and told me she'd explain to everyone what happened. That's what we did during seventh period. We simply discussed what had happened instead of listening during class.

"So how did your hands get wet? I thought they *couldn't* get wet," Sabrina asked.

"Well, they can't get wet unless I let them. Still, that

wasn't water on my hands. The girl dropped some kind of gel on her own head and somehow got it on my hands."

"Really?"

"Yup."

"So, what were you smiling about when you sat down?" I asked her.

"Oh, nothing. I just heard the girl laughing on her way out, so I sent a real water bubble her way."

We started giggling, yet the teacher didn't turn in our direction. In fact, we spent that entire class ignoring the teacher, and he ignored us right back. None of us got infractions, yet when we left the classroom, none of us were happy.

"Are you kidding me?!"

"We try our best to do everything right. What happens? We all get detention!"

"We completely ignore the teacher and do everything *wrong*?"

"Nothing! Not even a scold!"

Who knew that *not* getting detention could make a person angrier than *getting* detention?

CHAPTER 18

Sabrina

W hen we got to my house, we were all pretty tired. Staying out of trouble can be exhausting, after all. We all threw ourselves onto the couch and rested until my grandma walked in. I asked her for any updates on the dean.

"Katara has been at the school all day, ensuring that you got detention. In fact, she saw to it that you five would be the only ones with her."

Well, that's just not fair. I thought to myself.

"Still, you all must train for your battle tomorrow."
She swiftly clapped her hands, and we were all suddenly off the couch and outside. We all fell to the ground, unprepared for the sudden transportation. Well, all except Charlotte, who simply hovered in the air. And Sam, who'd turned into a smoke cloud upon impact.

"Alright, children! No more lollygagging, we've got work to do!"

Grandma cast her spell, and boulders rose from the ground.

"I've prepared a simulation to test your ability to work together."

The rocks began spinning rapidly around us.

"Keep in mind, you must also be able to take down Katara in the process. In this exercise, I will be playing the role of Katara."

She held up a necklace with a small rock dangling from it.

"Your goal is to take this necklace from me without completely destroying it."

She tied the necklace around her neck.

"Ready? Begin!"

The rocks immediately began hurling themselves towards us.

Instinctively, Sam and I rushed forward and blasted them as they came from all directions. The blasts caused dust to fill our area. When I looked up again, I could only see Sam behind me, but I heard Alex calling out to the others.

"Here, guys!" he shouted through the dust.

I wanted to turn and look for him, and I had to have his back. His and everyone else's.

"C'mon!" I called to Sam.

Together, we raced around the rest of the group. Following their voices through the dust. I dashed to the front, to make sure that no boulders got too close to my friends. Lightning cracked, and fires burned as stones were destroyed with ease. Soon, I saw my grandma ahead of me, and I fell back. The others burst through the dust, and all went for her at different angles. Without flinching, a rock wall quickly rose around her like a small cell.

That's when I saw Sam, getting ready to burn his way through.

"Wait! We can't blast the wall in!"

Everyone stopped.

"What! Why?" Sam asked.

"Because! If we did that, we'd most likely destroy the necklace in the process," Charlotte said.

And she's still my freaking Grandmother! *Not the real dean!* I thought to myself.

"Do we have any other options?" Sam asked.

"Maybe we could just crack the rock?" Alex suggested. "With my vines?"

"Then I could fill it with water! It could seep through the cracks." Eliza added.

"Afterwards, I would shock the whole thing, electrocuting the dean...*but* the dean isn't in there. My Grandma is."

"Right...so now what?" Eliza asked.

"Alex, can you grow vines through the *inside* of the wall?" Charlotte asked.

"Um...I think so," Alex put his hands on the ground and closed his eyes. After a few moments, he opened them and looked up at Charlotte.

"Okay, now what?"

"Crack the rock by pushing *outward*," she paused. "and grab the 'dean' if you can."

Alex nodded and closed his eyes again. We looked up when we heard the stone begin to crack. Alex strained to spread the vines out, and I could tell he was starting to get tired. That's when Charlotte flew up on top of the cell and put her hands on the growing cracks. Suddenly, gusts of air began spewing from every crack in the rock. They began to get bigger and bigger until the whole enclosure burst apart. In a split second, I'd moved everyone out of the way of the explosion before the rock pieces could hurt anyone.

When the dust cleared, I saw Charlotte and Alex laying in the grass, and I heard my grandma laughing. I looked up to see what was so funny, and saw that she was being suspended about four feet in the air by vines. I turned back to Alex and saw him smiling at her, laughing a bit himself. He had one hand in the grass and the other holding Charlotte's.

We went inside and rested for a while and took turns asking grandma questions.

"Why do we have to get the dean's necklace again?" Sam asked.

"You see, the ancient magic that Katara had millions of years ago was lost when her last asteroid struck the Earth. That magic was transferred to one of her asteroids and back to the Earth. It came to form what is known as an elemental stone.

Elemental stones hold amazing powers and are the key to unlocking special tools to help you defend the Earth. However, Katara's stone will likely be deformed and corrupted now due to the dark magic used to bring her back. It still lies within her stone, which is why it is crucial that you don't break it. If you do, the dark magic will be released and wreak havoc on Earth."

"Alright. Keep the necklace intact. Got it," Sam said, mentally taking notes.

"So, is that why we have all of these powers? Because of the elemental stones?" Eliza asked.

"Not exactly. You five were *born* with these elemental abilities. Most magicians are, but not everyone can control them without the use of their wands. The elemental *stones* will help you unlock new kinds of powers later on."

"What kind of powers?" Alex asked.

"Nobody knows..." Grandma said with an attempted dramatic effect. I was almost one hundred percent certain that if I did a quick search in her office, I would find a book that told us everything we needed to know, but I was pretty exhausted.

"Okay, well...we should go home now. We do have a massive battle tomorrow," Charlotte said as she began packing up her things.

I hadn't even noticed her wake up.

"Oh! You're right! I hadn't even noticed the time!"

Everyone was about to leave when Grandma stopped Sam and Charlotte.

"Hold on... Where did you get those?" she asked, pointing at their bracelets.

"This? My mom gave it to me when I was ten," Charlotte said.

"Same here," Sam said.

"Why, these are fragments of the shadow and spirit element stones!"

"Wait, what?" They said together.

"Yes, yes! This is incredible! I've got to find that book!" My grandma was about to run down to her office, but I grabbed her by the sleeve.

"Grandma, it's been a long day. Maybe we can do this to-morrow?"

She paused, looked back at our exhausted faces, and sighed.

"You're right. You all go get your rest. You have a big day ahead of you."

With that, everyone got their things and left. I went to bed before dinner, completely wiped out, and wondered what tomorrow had in store for us.

CHAPTER 19

Elizabeth

The next morning, I woke up in a cold sweat. I'd dreamt about the dean trying to smash me with her boulders. I dodged and dodged until one finally got me. Well, it got me awake, at least. I sighed and got ready for school with dread. Alex seemed exhausted from our fight the day before, but it was nothing compared to Charlotte. She plopped into her seat and almost immediately fell asleep. She didn't have her glasses, and her hair was a mess.

"Didn't sleep well, huh?"

She shook her head.

I sat next to her, took out my wand, and began stroking it over her hair.

"Look. I know you're exhausted, so I'm gonna let you rest. I'll brush your hair, and get you all cleaned up. Okay?" She nodded before she began to snore. I couldn't help but laugh while I let my wand work its magic. By the time we got to school, Charlotte looked well-rested and ready to face the day. At least until we woke her up. She still didn't have much energy, but at least she was presentable. We went to our lockers when Sam suddenly came out of nowhere and slammed into them.

He slumped over and began rubbing his forehead.

"Sam!" I knelt by his side. "Are you okay?"

He looked up at me, and I got a good look at him. His forehead was red, but there weren't any bruises. On the other hand, his hair was an absolute wreck, and I saw bags under his eyes.

"Lemme guess. You didn't sleep well?"

He nodded, and I began to laugh.

"Okay. Let's get you to homeroom," I said as I helped him up.

I led him to class and sat him down in his seat. Once we were seated, I had Alex grow the energy herb he'd given to me a few days before. I gave it to Sam and Charlotte, but they were hesitant.

"C'mon, guys. It'll get you wide awake and full of energy. It's...kinda like coffee."

It wasn't more than a second after I'd said the C-word that they were both eating the herb. Then Sabrina walked through the door, holding a cup with a cover over it.

When she walked over, Alex asked her what it was.

"This? It's a tea my grandma made. It replenishes energy and stimulates the senses!"

"Do you think we can have some?" Charlotte asked.

"Please?" Sam added.

"Um...I don't have anything to pour it in."

"Wait, maybe I can try something," I said.

Sabrina passed me her cup, and I took off the lid. I concentrated, envisioning the tea as a floating bubble-like liquid in space. After a moment. The entire cup of tea was now a floating bubble in my hands. I split the bubble into three slightly smaller ones and put one back in Sabrina's cup.

"Here!" I said, holding a floating tea bubble out to Sam and Charlotte.

Without hesitation, they slurped up the bubbles, and I saw the bags under their eyes disappear. They smiled and thanked Sabrina while she finished what was left of her tea.

For just about the whole day, nobody paid attention in class. We all just fooled around with our magic. I made bubbles, Charlotte made twisters, Sam made fire, Alex grew vines. Sabrina even made lightning bolts between her hands. None of the teachers seemed to notice or care enough to stop us, so we just kept at it.

During second period, however, we used the puzzles to ease our minds. We won again, and nobody accused us of cheating. It felt good to win, and for a little while, I forgot about the fight with our dean.

At lunch, we all focused on getting our homework done. Nobody spoke except for when we cast the spell on our lunches and the occasional question or two. But for the last two periods, we were as anxious as ever. I almost drenched a table after Sam lit it on fire. Alex started growing vines on the walls, and Sabrina almost struck us with her lightning, then Charlotte's twisters nearly got out of control.

At the end of the day, we all went back to homeroom in complete silence. Maybe ten minutes or so passed before a voice came over the intercom. *At this time, all students who received detention this week report to the dean's office.* We all rose and left homeroom. Students stared at us as we walked through the halls, but I didn't care. They didn't know that we were about to take this dean down *and* save the world. When we got to her office, she was just sitting at her desk. Waiting for us.

"So, you're the troublemakers?" she asked while keeping her gaze fixed on Alex and me.

"This is going to be very fun," she said with a malicious grin.

CHAPTER 20

Samuel

One minute, we were in the dean's office. The next...

"In a classroom?" I asked aloud.

"Well, it *is* still detention," Alex unnecessarily reminded me.

I began to look around.

"Where are we?"

"This looks like the abandoned school by the forest," Eliza announced.

"Yep. There's a forest," Sabrina said, looking out of a window.

"So...are we gonna battle or...?"

"I guess we'll have to wait," Charlotte said, lying on the floor with her feet flat against the wall. Well, ...she was actually hovering mid-air in the same position.

Let me tell you. I did not go through all of that training every day, lose sleep every night afterward, and slam into a locker door while walking through shadows to have *actual* detention for things that we didn't even have control over.

"This is ridiculous! We went through all of that training for a real battle just to get locked in a classroom?!"

"Well, the door could be *unlocked*," Charlotte said as she hovered by.

I walked up to the door, and before I could grab the handle, it swung open.

Coventina and Pan, please step into the hallway. A voice echoed throughout the room. Alex and Eliza exchanged worried glances.

"Don't worry! We're right behind you!" Charlotte said reassuringly.

They smiled and walked out into the hallway. We started after them, but the door slammed shut behind them.

"Hey!" I shouted.

Sabrina began tugging on the doorknob.

"It's locked."

"Not for long..." I grumbled. I grabbed the knob with both hands and melted it off. Then I pushed hard against the door until it opened. When it did, we burst out into the hallway and saw Alex and Eliza in a large stone cage, both arms bound in stone behind their backs.

"Well look who decided to join the party!" the sorceress said.

"Let them go," Sabrina demanded.

The dean scoffed, "Who are you to tell me how to utilize my prisoners?"

She sent three flying boulders our way.

Sabrina and I blasted two, but the third one headed straight for Charlotte. Before she could react, I saw the boulder slam right into her, leaving nothing but a poof of dust behind.

"Charlotte!" Alex screamed in disbelief.

"No..." I heard Eliza murmur.

Sabrina gritted her teeth, "You're gonna pay for that."

She sent thousands of gigavolts of lightning towards the dean, but she just blocked it with a stone wall where it only left a few cracka. I dove through the shadows to get behind her. Once hit her in the back with a flaming fisted punch. She crashed into her wall, breaking it. I stood over her, ready to finish the job when a boulder came out of nowhere and clocked me in the noggin.

I grabbed my head in my hands, wanting to scream.

*Sam...*I heard a voice say.

Saaaam...Sam!

I looked up and saw a wispy figure in front of me.

"Oh, no. I couldn't have died!"

What? No, you didn't die! You're still in this! I need you to help me free the others.

The wispy figure's voice sounded familiar but distant. It echoed through my head as it spoke, and its overall figure seemed to waver every few seconds. I quickly followed it behind the stone cage as I tried to rub away the pounding aches in my head. I wasn't sure if I'd been hit too hard and was hallucinating, but I didn't have time to worry about it. I looked up and saw Alex, who had managed to break apart his bonds, was furiously slashing the bars with his vines, but they stayed intact. Eliza was sitting on the ground, silent. Her arms still bound behind her back.

"Alex! Stop! You're just going to wear yourself out!" I called to him

"I don't care! I'll get her. For what she did to Charlotte!!"

I thought I saw tears streaming down his cheeks.

He didn't stop slashing, and the wispy figure just looked up at him. Before I could ask it for a plan, it flew up to Alex. I heard it calmly shush him until he finally fell to his knees.

It's okay. I'm here. It said calmly.

The wisp suddenly turned back to me and nodded, keeping one hand on Alex's shoulder. I nodded back and blew the back of the cage apart. Alex looked back, and when he saw me, he smiled.

I broke off Eliza's bonds, and soon the twins joined the fight. Together we quickly began to tire out the sorceress. Soon, once we'd surrounded her, she summoned a stone wall as a barrier around herself.

"We've practiced this, guys. Alex? You're up."

He just stood there. Staring at the wall.

"Um... Alex?" Eliza said, putting a hand on his shoulder.

He balled up his fists and grew thick, thorny vines. He slashed at the rock over and over and over again, until it began to crack.

"Alex! What are you doing?!" Sabrina demanded.

He didn't answer her. He just turned to me.

"I need you to fill those cracks with smoke."

"Uh...sure." I walked up to the wall and put my hands on the cracks. I closed my eyes and focussed, letting smoke pour through each one.

I began to hear the sorceress cough inside her wall. She choked and hacked, and eventually, she stopped. Then the wall collapsed, leaving a cloud of dust. There she lay in a crumpled heap on the ground.

"She's not...we didn't...is she okay?" Sabrina managed.

"I-I'm not sure," I stuttered.

That's when I saw the wispy figure again. It flew to the dean's side and laid its hands over her mouth. Suddenly, the dean began coughing again.

"Quick! Her necklace!" Eliza said.

Sabrina quickly snatched the necklace off of the dean's neck as she kept choking. Sabrina's grandma had been right about it being corrupted. It was twisted and contorted unnaturally. I could even see the dark magic swirling within it, writhing in search of escape.

Alex quickly grabbed her with some of his vines and held her up in the air. The dean suddenly opened her eyes and glared at us furiously.

"Release me at once, you stupid brats!"

"Heh. Whatever you say," I said while winking to Sabrina.

Alex glared at her before setting her back down on the ground. Before she could move, Sabrina shocked her with a few of her lightning bolts. Stunned, the dean fell to the ground.

"Well. That sure was *shocking*!" I said, making everyone laugh. Even the wisp. That's when I noticed something incredibly familiar about the wisp. Its laugh seemed kind of young and cute. Its hair was curly but poofy, and it kind of reminded me of...

"Charlotte?!"

Acknowledgements

To start, I owe infinite thanks to both my mom and dad for helping me find the resources needed to make this dream a reality. Even when it seemed like the writing would never end, my parents stuck by me. They used my determination to push me and helped me finish this story by my thirteenth birthday. However, there would be no story if there had been no idea, for which I have to thank my close friend Sophie Lee. As I recall, this story came into the world on a sunny spring afternoon during our time in the after school program. We came up with several ideas that day but I remembered *Magic C.A.S.E.S.* being discussed as our original storyline. A story about two soon-to-be wizards named Charlotte and Sabrina.

Of course several changes were made, but I was sure to keep key aspects of our original characters the same, as well as adding new traits to them. They will continue to grow close to each other as friends, but there will also be others that they will grow even closer to. In the end, I am looking forward to writing another book, and more to come in the future. Still, for now I am certainly proud of how far I have come as both a person and a creator.

Made in the USA
Columbia, SC
01 December 2019